I ONCE
WAS
LOST

Fr Lapera)
Thank you For All your
Effort To Engage
The "Thomas" Character

JONATHAN FANNING

Jonathan Fanning

I ONCE WAS LOST

FIRST EDITION
Copyright ©2018 Jonathan Fanning

ISBN
978-164316986-6

Cover Design: Rebecca Lazaroff

For more information on this title and other books, videos,
CDs, seminars, and speaking engagements, please visit:
www.JonathanFanning.com

Printed in the United States of America.

Contents

Why Ask Why?

Aslan: "Do you feel yourself sufficient to take up the Kingship of Narnia?"
Caspian: "I - I don't think that I do, sir. I'm only a kid."
Aslan: "Good. If you had felt yourself sufficient, it would have been proof that you were not."

Once upon a time there was a young man who thought he had everything figured out – that is, before realizing that he had absolutely nothing figured out. You are in this story. So am I. This is the story about the influence of a six-year-old child and a fairy tale on that young man.

What's the point? What are we doing here? Why learn this? Why? Why? Why? These are questions he would ask in history class, in high school algebra, in calculus, physics, chemistry, German. He would ask his teachers, sports coaches, and parents. Did he get a satisfactory answer? No one seemed quite sure. He'd even asked these questions sometimes on Sundays. Shall we join him on a small – yet incredibly significant – segment of his journey?

Ironically, it was an absolutely gorgeous Friday afternoon when the entire world collapsed around Thomas. It seems there are so many ways for the whole world to fall apart. As Thomas drove rather aimlessly away from everything that had mattered to him, the clichés – too many clichés – spun around in his head, echoing louder and more intense, then softer, then louder and louder again, more and more intense. Their grip on his mind was firm. The clichés were shared through so many different voices... "If this is the worst that's ever happened to you", "count your blessings", "you've got so many good things going for you", "it's not the end of the world", all these thoughts... But the world – his world – had absolutely collapsed. There was no purpose. There was no reason. No hope.

1

Where could he go? Where could one go under the circumstances? Home was not a very good option. On a long drive? No! To a town park that should be quite empty until the school day ends? Yes. That must be the answer. And that's how Thomas found himself sitting alone on a green, well-used park bench along the river early on a beautiful Friday afternoon. He stared towards nothing, towards no one. He was alone with his thoughts and they were not the best of company. He was somehow wanting an answer, wanting guidance, but at this moment Thomas was certain about only one thing. There was no answer, there was no guidance, there was no point.

In this moment, the old self-assured Thomas seemed to never have existed. But it really wasn't so long ago. The old Thomas questioned everything with a sense of authority, approached new information and challenges with a cockiness, a sense that if there was something to figure out, he would most certainly figure it out. He not only knew everything, but he knew that he knew everything. That Thomas was great at giving advice and great at deciding which advice to apply. But, in this moment, he felt none of that confidence, none of his trademark certainty. It had all disappeared, vanished without a trace. Not slowly. Not gradually. It was just gone.

"Snap out of it! Thomas! Snap out of it!" he thought to himself. This had always worked, had always been his solution. If ever some part of his world seemed to come a little bit unhinged, or go a little bit off course from his carefully orchestrated design, if his feathers had ever gotten ruffled, he would just yank himself back out of it, set a new and very clear direction, and get to work. Get to work. That was the answer. Or was it? Somehow, this time seemed different. This time seemed to have more finality. Thomas had always told himself that he would do some incredible things in his life. So many people around him had validated this belief. He was ahead of the curve, he was a mover and a shaker, accomplishing big

things at a young age. But right now, in this moment, that seemed like a completely made up story. It seemed as if everything was for nothing.

As Thomas stared blankly, but intently, from that bench, he pondered: if getting back to work wasn't the answer, if setting a new clear direction, lowering his head and charging wasn't the answer, what was? He'd always like that Harry Chapin song with the refrain *all my life's a circle and I can't tell you why*. Somehow that refrain just seemed to be spinning 'round again and again and again inside his head. *All my life's a circle and I can't tell you why. Season's spinning 'round again and the years keep rolling by.*

For a split second, just a moment, he actually thought about that bridge. So many had used the famous bridge in an attempt to end their despair. Just imagining it caused a shudder through his whole body. Thomas had to grit his teeth and said *no, no, NO! I don't! Not me! I don't even think those thoughts*! But he had. And it wasn't the first time. How could he even try to describe the multiple feelings that washed over him? Feelings of guilt, remorse, anger, confusion, sadness, hopelessness. But the one that seemed to worry him the most at this moment was a feeling of relief. He had thought about the bridge and then had felt relief.

How could that ever be the answer – for anyone? But Thomas grabbed on to that idea for a moment... Or maybe that idea grabbed onto him. That was certainly what it felt like to Thomas.

"Good afternoon." It came from a soft, but deep, calm and soothing voice on Thomas's left. "Good afternoon." A bit louder this time. "Do mind if I join you?"

This interruption to his thoughts took Thomas back to a hundred memories of his childhood.

"Earth to Thomas! Earth to Thomas!"

"Ground control to Major Tom!"

"Welcome back, Tom!"
"Thank you for joining us, Tommy!"
"Thomas, was there something you wanted to add or ask?"
"Thomas, are you with us?"
"Tommy, you have quite an active imagination..."

As a young boy, and even into his teen years, Thomas had spent a significant amount of time living an imagined life. He was the race car driver, the pitcher in the World Series, the pinch hitter, the inventor, the great explorer, the daring hero, the admired leader, the first ever to accomplish something (you name it!), the one with the answers. Sometimes, the imagined life had seemed more real, more meaningful, more substantial, than his actual experiences.

"Tommy, you're in at 2nd base." It was the fourth inning of a little league all-star game. Second base? As a *substitute* in the fourth inning? Something didn't line up. Something was wrong with this script. Tommy was a starter. He was going to break all the records. He would turn down astronomical salaries so that ordinary families could still afford to come out to the ballpark to see him play. Other players and even owners would follow his incredible example. But here, today, on this beautiful summer afternoon, Tommy – at the age of 12 – is a substitute at second base and batting 9th. After two innings with limited activity on defense, Tommy sprinted off the field and grabbed a helmet and bat. His chance to shine and correct this whole scenario had arrived. The first batter laced a double into the left field gap. Tommy walked to the plate, but in his mind, this was not just a little league all-star game. It was bigger. This was October baseball in the big leagues. Kids around the country were allowed to stay up late to watch the greatest baseball players on the greatest stage. For Thomas, the imagined life is about to collide with a harsh reality.
"Strike one!"

Wow! That was fast! Tommy thought to himself. The pitcher's motion was deceptive, and Tommy had just taken a very good pitch to hit. But he was ready now, and took a big swing at the next pitch, even though it was at least a foot above the strike zone. No contact.

"Strike two! No balls, two strikes," the umpire called out.

"Let's go Tommy, put it in play!" came the cheers from the stands and the bench.

The next pitch was a little bit outside, but Thomas wasn't about to let another ball go by, so he lunged awkwardly, just barely making enough contact to foul the ball back into the screen.

"Hey now, Tommy. Come on Tommy... We need this one!"

Tommy's mind began to race. On one hand, he was sure he would come through. But on the other, he could feel every eye on him. He was batting 9th, after all, and the *substitute* second baseman. The next pitch bounce before it reached home plate, but Tommy panicked and almost made an offering at this unhittable ball. This was not the way it was supposed to go. Somehow, the cool, calm, collected Tommy seemed not to be in control of this at-bat. The next pitch would be the last one that Tommy would remember from this game. It would be a pitch that he'd remember for weeks and weeks afterwards. It was a fastball up and in, outside of the strike zone and not a pitch he had any business swinging at. Tommy did swing and then the boy walked a lonely walk back to the dugout.

"Strike three!"

Where could he go from here? Where? The point of his life was athletic endeavor, not just endeavor, success. Success – this word would come back to challenge and confuse him.

"Do mind if I join you?" The deep, soothing voice brought Thomas back to his park bench and reality.

"Sure, but I don't know if I'll be much company this afternoon," Thomas mumbled, without even looking up.

After a few moments of silence, the deep voice asked, "What are you looking for?" This was an odd way to begin a conversation, but the question hung in the air, and carried a deep sincerity.

"Huh?" was about all Thomas could utter in response. Was he looking for something? Had he been thinking out loud? An instant ago, Thomas was thinking of walking away, with a simple excuse that he had to be somewhere. That question – and the way it was asked – pinned him to the bench. It was not a fair question to ask. Not now. Not after Thomas had actually been contemplating the point, or lack-there-of, of everything in his life. He wasn't looking for anything. He, Thomas, has seriously entertained the bridge. Who would really miss him? Is that why this question was asked? Did this stranger see Thomas looking off in the distance towards the bridge? Maybe changing the subject would be best. That was Thomas's plan, but that's not how the words came out.

"I really don't know anymore. I've always known, but right now, I just don't know." Thomas looked up as these strange words came out of his mouth.

"What an incredible day! What a gift! Please allow an old man to rest his weary body and enjoy the pleasure of your company. The name's Joseph."

"Thomas."

As they shook hands, Thomas realized that Joseph was a mountain of a man. He took a seat on Thomas' bench. His powerful presence made Thomas think he must have earned his wisdom. Something about Joseph, more than just his size, reminded Thomas of the large inmate, John Coffee, from the movie *The Green Mile*.

"I once was lost," the big man words were deep but soft as his gaze drifted across the river.

Thomas didn't respond. Really, he couldn't. He wasn't sure that he'd actually heard these words out loud.

"Most of us… have been. If… if we only knew… what… we were *supposed* to be looking for… that changes *everything*." The

6

old man spoke slowly, deliberately, as if reminding himself of a long, meaningful, and almost forgotten chapter of his own life.

"Yeah, I hear you." Thomas mumbled. How else does one respond when overhearing another's mysterious reflections?

Joseph's eyes were closed, and when he opened them, they seemed to have changed. There was an energy and fiery intensity in them now. "Do you have a favorite author?" Thomas didn't respond, but that didn't seem to bother the old man. "What are you reading these days? Whose words do you allow to affect your life?" The stranger must have interpreted Thomas' body language as permission to continue. "Centuries ago, a contemporary of Socrates known as Damon of Athens wisely said, '*Let me write the songs of a nation, and I care not who writes its laws.*' Do tell me, young Thomas, what songs do you let guide your thoughts?"

"Joseph, while I appreciate your question and philosophical dialogue, I'm a businessman. I wish I had time for books, songs, poetry, philosophy. About the only books I read deal with business strategy, marketing, finance…"

Joseph made a quick glance towards the ground as he heard these words, as if to say, "Tis a shame." But he didn't say it. There was no need to express the words aloud.

"I see." The man paused, and Thomas felt uncomfortable under the weight of these two simple words. Did this man really see? Did he see all the mess of emotions and thoughts Thomas was trying so desperately to hide? "If you're up to a challenge… May I recommend a book?"

"Bring it on!" Thomas had used this expression so many times, but this time, his words lacked conviction.

When Thomas' cell phone abruptly interrupted the moment, vibrating with unanswered messages, Thomas was jolted right back into his standard routine. He rudely turned his attention to the phone, scanned through the messages and sent a few rushed responses.

Meaningful conversations rarely even made it this far. Thomas was a busy man, always getting things done, and didn't have time for these poetic and philosophical conversations.

"I gotta hit the road. Sorry to rush off, but I'm sure you understand. Good talking with you." He spoke with an indifference that even surprised himself. "I'll see you around." Thomas stood up and nodded at the big man.

"You will." Joseph's massive left hand rested firmly on Thomas's shoulder and the two men clasped hands firmly.

As Thomas walked back to his car, he realized that no other benches in the park had been occupied. Why did this Joseph sit by him? When he started the car, a crumpled piece of paper dropped out of his right hand. Just a few letters were scribbled on it. The old man must have pressed it into his hand as they departed. Those letters were about to change everything.

7 letters

Two days later, Thomas hopped in the car and quickly sped to the grocery store to pick up a few last-minute items. He parked the car at the grocery store and grabbed the empty coffee cup to discard as he entered the store. Like everything else in his life, he liked his car clean and orderly. Under the cup was a little scrap of paper. Thomas took that, as well. He tossed the cup into the garbage, but held on to that little scrap, vaguely remembering that the paper held some importance. He didn't waste any time in the grocery store. He never did. Wasting time was for other people. Bread, check. Milk, check. Pasta, check. Veggies, check. Fresh corn, check. Cold cuts, no! Never mind. There was a line for the deli. Thomas stood there for a moment and considered leaving. He wasn't one to wait patiently on lines of any sort. But today, for a change, the line was moving rather quickly. He joined the line and took that small crumpled piece of paper out of his pocket. Seven lower case letters, hand-written with an impressive old English penmanship style:

lewiscs

He tried to fit the letters into his conversation with Joseph, the conversation he had been unable to get out of this head for the last 48 hours, even though it couldn't have lasted more than a few short minutes. It was ended so abruptly by Thomas's normal routine of excusing himself whenever a discussion went in a direction that he didn't favor. Why had such a brief interaction – with so few words exchanged and no business importance – left such an imprint on him? And what did these letters mean? Thomas tried to replay the conversation in his mind and was surprised at how much was still clear to him. Not just clear, burning, seared into his memory. There was that bold question, still begging a response: "What are you looking for?" The wise stranger had said something about knowing what we're *supposed* to be looking for. What exactly does that mean? This stranger, this Joseph. Thomas wondered what his angle could be. What was this Joseph character looking for? That should have been Thomas's response. But somehow the questions, or maybe the way they were asked, had caught Thomas off guard. Why was this crumpled piece of paper in his hand after their conversation? He turned the paper over and over in his hands, looking at the letters forward, backward, upside down. He was looking for something but not exactly sure what.

"Hey, pal, what can we get for you?" For once, the man at the deli was waiting on Thomas, instead of the other way around.

Thomas ordered his cold cuts and headed home. His little sister was coming over for a barbecue that afternoon, and he could take up this mystery with her. She had always liked mysteries.

"Tiff, I met your kind of guy the other day at the park." They had just finished a mouthwatering meal on Thomas's back patio. Steak, corn on the cobb, marinated vegetables, and rosemary potatoes, all dripping with the flavor and anticipation of an early spring barbecue. Thomas brought out a plate of assorted Italian cookies and two homemade cappuccinos.

"Oh yeah? And what exactly is my kind of guy? And since when do I need you to pick up a guy for me at the park?" Tiffany was still not ready to date again, or at least that had been her line for a while now.

Thomas ignored the comment and the brief glimpse of sadness that flashed across his sister's face.

"Philosopher, poet, deep thinker."

"So, you were paying me a compliment... Thank you!" Tiff shot back.

"Sure. Wish you could have been there. The two of you could have traded meaningless quotes from ancient history." Thomas's sarcasm was nothing out of the ordinary.

"Please tell me that you had a conversation with him – that you didn't just dismiss my new boyfriend!" Despite being the younger sister, Tiff had a history of offering unsolicited, but often quite helpful, motherly guidance. She had tremendous respect for her big brother. Sure, she could tease with the best, but she also seemed to know when it was her time to look out for him. "What quotes did he share with you?"

"Oh, I don't know." Thomas feigned indifference. "something about songs-writers making the laws."

"Well that's certainly the kind of profound statement I should expect from my future husband! Brilliant, simply brilliant."

Thomas looked like he was deep in thought and that got Tiff's attention. Then, with closed eyes, he slowly and softly recited: "His wording was more powerful: 'Let me write the songs of a nation...'"

"...and I care not who writes its laws." Tiffany finished the sentence with him.

They locked eyes for just a moment and Tiffany saw something in her brother that she had not seen in a very long time. He was searching. He didn't know the answer. He was humble. He was afraid. His path forward was covered in a dense fog. Tiffany felt compelled to slide around the table and hug her big brother.

Thomas normally didn't let these moments last. He was definitely not a hugger. But on this night, Tiff's embrace provided just enough warmth, just enough hope, that things might somehow turn out okay.

"What did the stranger do with my brother?" Tiff knew her brother well enough to know that this moment might not last and might not come back. She would seize this moment.

"He challenged me. I don't even know who he is. I know nothing about his background. As far as I know, he doesn't know anything about me, either. But when he asked me whose words and what songs I let affect my life, I could tell that he actually cared about the answer. It was more than just an answer that he cared about. I guess the only way I could describe it just to say that I could

11

tell he cared about me, or the impact that these songs might have on me. I don't know. I don't know what I'm trying to describe." Thomas's voice trailed off with a hesitancy that worried Tiff.

"Do you..." Thomas interrupted Tiff before she even decided on a question.

"I almost forgot! What do you make of this?" He let the crumpled paper fall on the table next to her biscotti.

"Is it a code?" Tiff wasn't sure if this was one of the classic 'change the conversation' maneuvers she had learned to dread from her brother.

"He gave it to me. It's part of our conversation, maybe the continuation of it, but I don't know what it means." He was marching around the patio now, with a familiar brisk walk that said he was going places, finding answers, solving problems, making things happen.

"It's a continuation!" Thomas blurted excitedly. "Joseph challenged me to read a book. I think he was writing something before I made up an excuse that I had to leave..."

Tiff almost toppled her cappuccino as she jumped out of her chair to interrupt. "I have to get something from my car." She practically sprinted to her car and returned with a stack of books.

Thomas really wanted to solve this, and was more than a little bit frustrated with his sister for her lack of focus. But she had a smile on her face, and he was happy to see this. For the last few months, she really had not been herself. Tiff dropped the stack of old books on the table, and this time her cappuccino spilled across everything, including one of the books. The response was both rapid and typical. Thomas lunged forward, grabbed the cup, moved the books, glared at his little sister in disgust, and opened his mouth to make one of his famous comments. But no words came out. His body froze, mouth still hanging open, and then slowly sank into his chair and began to shake his head back and forth in disbelief. He turned the coffee stained book over in his hands several times, flipped through a few pages and then, with the bewildered look Tiff had seen so frequently when they were children, her brother reached across the table and handed her the book.

"The Lion..., the Witch..., and the Wardrobe by C.S. Lewis! *'lewiscs'* He's the answer? Joseph challenged me to read a children's book?"

Tiff was smiling, not a smile of pure joy, but one mixed with deep sadness. "I finally picked them up a few days ago from Paul's parents." Her words were slow and controlled. Even though Thomas was by no means a master of compassion, he knew that his sister needed time, needed patience. But his mind was racing, trying to decipher the giant man's intentions with this reading challenge. Tiff breathed very slowly, and her voice trembled as she continued her thought, "He told Ryan they would read them all together when he was 6." She couldn't continue, but closed her eyes tightly, took a few shallow breathes, and her voice quivered on, "Ryan's...6th birthday is... is... Tuesday." She was sobbing now, her whole body shuddering, and her breathing matched her heart rate – irregular, loud, rapid.

"I'll do it." Thomas heard his own words and knew it was the right thing to say. He never seemed to deal with these situations well, but this was authentic. He pulled his little sister close to him and whispered with conviction, "I'll read the books with him."

Tiffany jumped up. "Ryan! I have to pick him up. What time is it?" She clutched her keys and ran towards her car.

"Tiff! Stay here. I'll get him. Take a few minutes off from being 'Super Mom.'" Before she could even respond, Thomas was speeding away in his BMW convertible.

So it Begins

Ryan was a great kid. Sure, he had his moments, but Thomas just adored that kid. Had it really been 6 years since Thomas' baby sister had become a mom? 6 years! On this beautiful Sunday afternoon, Ryan was playing at a friend's house, and on the drive over, Thomas thought about all the times when he had committed to becoming a bigger part of this little guy's life. There were so many: the first time he held little Ryan in the hospital, when Ryan learned to walk and suddenly became much more like a little person, when that little fella suddenly started communicating with opinions and questions of his own, the day Paul had announced that he would be deployed to the Middle East, when Ryan brought home a stick figure drawing of his family that included Thomas, that September afternoon at Ryan's first professional baseball game, and the painful months after Paul's return from active duty.

Unfulfilled promises. This time would be different. That's what Thomas told himself, but almost immediately realized that this phrase was like the kiss of death to every new promise. Hadn't he said that each time? Life's betrayed promises bombarded Thomas's thoughts as his convertible took a hard turn a little bit faster than the warning signs recommended.

It is what it is. You have to do what you have to do. That's life. Success has a price tag.

Tired clichés. The tires screeched as Thomas slammed on the brakes! He pulled off to the side of the road for just a moment, pounded on the steering wheel, and promised himself that this time really *would* be different. Some of these ridiculous clichés that Thomas uttered so often would have to go. Where they part of the "songs of the nation" Joseph had mentioned? A strange peace washed away the anger that Thomas felt for letting these misguided *songs* guide his life. Thomas drove on in a unique emotional state

– a peaceful intensity – about this renewed commitment to his nephew.

"Uncle Tommy!!" No one else got away with calling him Tommy these days. The little guy ran around the side of his best friend's house as soon as he saw the car turn into the driveway. How could you do anything but smile when you saw so much joy on this child's face? By the time Ryan reached the car, Uncle Tommy was standing in the driveway. They both laughed with that contagious laughter of two mischievous kids as they pounded fists in their customary greeting. Ryan tilted his head to the side and nodded a few times with his 'cool guy' grin.

"I-C-E… C-R-E-…" Thomas didn't get to finish spelling before Ryan was climbing into the convertible – without opening the door. Tiff would not approve of the climbing, but Ryan had that simple wisdom to know his audience!

"Yeah, of course! Just me and you, Uncle Tommy? I'll share it with you. Chocolate and vanilla, right? Can I drive? I want to sit on your lap to back out of the driveway. Then I'll drive from the backseat. I'm Luke Skywalker. Uncle Tommy, you're on my team. You can be, um, what was his name?"

"Han. Han Solo." Thomas had to smile. He had played the same way. It was a lifetime ago, but the joy of an unfettered imagination was still in there, somewhere.

Ryan sat on his uncle's lap as they backed out of the driveway. Then Ryan climbed into the backseat, waved bye to his friend and called out, "I use the force to drive from the back seat. Watch this!" Ryan's hand was out and every muscle on the left side of his body seemed to be clenched in order to give the car its commands. Ryan's friend was in awe as the car obeyed and sped away.

Thomas knew his sister might not have been thrilled that the boys had watched a few Star Wars movies together, but she had been a good sport. Besides, she loved when her brother made time for her little guy. It was so good for both of them, but all too rare with Thomas's business and busyness.

A few minutes later they pulled into a parking spot at the ice cream shop. Ryan raised his hand, turned his head to the side, and made the face of an extremely focused Young Skywalker.

"I did good, right Uncle Tommy?"

"Yeah, you did better than good. You saved the galaxy, young Jedi!" Thomas said in his deepest narrator voice.

Within minutes, they were sitting on that same park bench, looking across the river and sharing the biggest ice cream cone Ryan had ever seen. Thomas set down his backpack, stuffed with a kickball, whiffle balls, two bats, water bottles, and a freshly coffee-stained old leather-bound book.

They passed the towering ice cream cone loaded with alternating scoops of vanilla and chocolate back and forth, talking about everything - from cartoons, to birds, to boats, to ants, to baseball, to foods mommy made Ryan "try before you cry!"

"Wanna see how far I can hit?"

"Sure! Let's see what you've got!" Thomas reminisced about how much he had always loved a challenge as a boy. Apparently, some things don't change! Whack! This little guy could really hit the ball. They took turns batting, if you could really call it taking turns. Ryan got a few dozen swings and then Uncle Tommy took about a half dozen.

"Yer out! Now batting for the New York..." Ryan announced as he ran off the pitcher's mound and took another turn in the batter's box. This game would go a full nine innings!

"I'm thirsty, Uncle Tommy."

Seated back on the bench, Ryan looked and hesitantly asked, "I hit pretty good, right?"

"You sure did, buddy! I can't believe how hard you hit the ball today."

"That's because I'm big. I'm 6. Well, almost 6. How many days?" Ryan's eyes rolled toward the sky as he tried to calculate the number of days before Tuesday. "You don't go to school on your birthday, do you? Daddy didn't go to work on his birthday. Remember?"

Thomas didn't respond. This day had more emotion than he had bargained for. He stood up slowly, lifting the backpack from the bench. "Ryan, I have a surprise for you. An early birthday gift."

"Really? Can I open it?" A smile returned to Ryan's sweaty face.

"Well, it's not exactly wrapped, but we can open it together. It's … umm… well, it's from your Dad." Thomas hadn't really planned what he would say about the gift. Together, they slowly pulled a book out of the backpack. This little guy was special. Thomas watched him hold the book, look at the cover, and open it. His eyes filled with a focused excitement, as they locked on a handwritten note on the inside of the cover.

"Paul! It says Paul. It's my daddy's name! He wrote me a note!"

"No, little buddy, let me see." Thomas took a few breaths and try to figure out what to say. Tiff would've known.

"Ryan, it's… it's a note *to* your daddy from *his* daddy."

Ryan searched for understanding.

"Let's read it together! Ryan, how about that, buddy?"

The little guy just nodded, looking like he was between smiling and tearing up. "Uh huh."

They worked through the words together:

Paul,
In these pages you will find a magical adventure and the answers
to many of life's questions. I love you forever and ever! Happy 6th
birthday!
Dad

That was a little more than Thomas had bargained for.

"Can you read it to me, Uncle Tommy?"

"You bet, Ryan. You bet."

Time disappeared as they began to read together that afternoon. Ryan migrated from sitting next to Uncle Tommy, to leaning his head on his uncle's arm, to sitting on his uncle's lap. The only interruptions came to send a text message to Tiff, letting her know that all was well, and for Ryan to ask an occasional question. When it was time to take Ryan home, the boy was very silent in the back seat of the car. Only after the car was stopped in front of Tiff's house, did the little guy finally speak up.

"I was thinking. Could we, I mean I know you're busy and all, but could we read more tomorrow?"

Before he even realized what he was saying, Thomas responded, "Of course we can!"

"Uncle Tommy, I want to... can we... do you think we can finish the whole book in two days, by my 6th birthday?"

"We will."

He watched the little guy's face light up before he turned to run into the house, clutching his special present.

"Love you, buddy!"

"Me too, Uncle Tommy!" Ryan shouted, between excitedly explaining to his mom in random order all that had happened that day.

Upside Down is Right Side Up

"Thanks! Are you sure?" That's all Tiff's text message said.

"Yes. This time, yes." Thomas replied almost instantly.

The next few weeks were a blur, but a very different blur than any Thomas had experienced before. That Friday afternoon call, the call that knocked his world to pieces, somehow seemed so insignificant, almost irrelevant. The investors had pulled the plug. Not all the investors, only the ones who still had money, the ones not named Thomas. After almost two years of 70- to 90-hour work weeks with very little pay and even less help, Thomas was the last man standing. But he wasn't standing. He was walking on air. Sure, the bills were piling up, and liquidating all the equipment didn't look like it would cover the failed start-up's debt. Everything in his world was wrong, but something felt completely right. Shutting down a failed start-up made for an extremely full schedule. Despite the time demands, Thomas had carved out at least one solid hour each and every day to be with his nephew, to really be with him. He had kept his promise this time. At least for now. To Tiff's great surprise, they did they finish that first book on Ryan's 6th birthday. That night, after cake and ice cream, they dove into the next book and read for at least an hour past bedtime. Tiff didn't make a comment. A few times, Thomas had noticed her standing in the doorway, just watching them with an aura of peace practically emanating from her face. Ryan was absolutely carried away by the adventures. So was Thomas. He even continued to read several pages before he realized that the birthday boy had fallen fast asleep. The facial expression on the boy didn't change. He looked like he was marching through the Narnian woods, meeting fantastic creatures, and preparing for the battle of his life.

"Thank you for doing this!" Tiff put two cups of tea on the kitchen table, offering Thomas a seat before heading home. "He's so into these stories with you! I don't know what to say. It means so much to him... and to me."

Thomas sipped his tea and thought about Ryan's enchantment. "It's been amazing. I didn't think he'd be so into the books. There's just something about the stories, or maybe the way they're told..." Her big brother paused, deep in thought, but his body didn't reflect his usual anxiety-filled quest for an immediate solution. He seemed okay with there just being "something" about the stories. "You know, you're not doing a bad job with him, little sister!" He finished his tea and walked towards the door. A lot of work awaited him still that night. As he opened the door, his sister whispered something that would captivate his thoughts for many days.

"The fingerprint of God."

"Huh," was all he said in response. "Goodnight, Tiff." The door closed.

A Great Adventure

For the next few weeks, a simple pattern repeated itself. Thomas didn't sleep much, but the sleep that he did get was much more peaceful and left him better rested then he remembered being in a long time. Each morning he arose extremely early and plowed through paperwork, contracts, legal documents, inventories. By 7:30 am, he'd be getting out of the car at Tiff's tiny apartment and sneaking into Ryan's room to wake him up. That only worked for a few days before Ryan was on to him. Then Ryan changed the game and would be in hiding before Uncle Tommy arrived. A few times, Ryan even snuck into his hiding spot the night before and slept there all night.

"I scared you, I scared you. Mom! I scared Uncle Tommy!" Tiff's face lit up to see her only child so excited about something again.

A pillow fight, or a game of hide-and-seek might follow. Thomas read out loud while Ryan ate breakfast, got his school clothes on, and brushed his teeth. By 8:30 they would be walking to school together. Tiff had been lucky to find this small apartment just a few blocks away from the elementary school.

"Aslan's always there." Ryan definitively announced one morning as they approached the school entrance.

"Yup." Thomas looked at the little guy and struggled for a few moments to stay present. After dropping off the first-grader, he would bury himself in business until 3:30 pickup, hang out with his nephew for two hours until Tiff got home, get back to his business shutdown action items, and try to make it back for Ryan's bedtime. Then he'd head home for another few hours of emails, contract analysis, evaluating offers on liquidating inventory and equipment. He was relieved that a woman he had been dating had decided that they needed some time apart, that they were looking for very different things.

Wait, that's it! Thomas almost said this aloud, but instead he asked a question. "What do you mean, buddy?

"He's just always there. It's like they might not see him 'cause he's hiding really good, but he always sees them. If they really need his help, he just jumps out of his hiding spot. Surprise!!! Like the way I get you every morning. Haha! Ha! I'm right here!"

"You and Aslan, you hide and surprise everyone!" He rubbed the little guy's mop of hair.

"Race you to the school, Uncle Tommy!" Ryan was off and running, those little legs seemed to have grown longer and become more coordinated overnight. The kid could run!

"Beat ya!" Ryan practically collided with the school door, but his victorious expression betrayed not a single sign of pain. "See ya later, Mr. Tumnus!" For several weeks after they read the first book, Ryan had taken to teasingly calling his uncle 'Mr. Tumnus', after the first character Lucy meets in Narnia. Then, the proud first-grader half-skipped, half-marched through the doorway and into the school.

Thomas just stood there, near the school entrance, with his hands behind his head and gazing off at the ominous gray sky. A thunderstorm was rapidly approaching. A few raindrops were already hitting him on the head. He didn't even know how long he had been standing there or when it started raining. Normally, he would be put off by this weather.

"Life." Thomas turned abruptly towards the voice. Her soft and nervous voice continued, "Life… is what you make of it."

The voice belonged to a young mother Thomas had seen dropping off a child at the school many times before. Her beat up old blue Toyota hatchback wasn't much to look at. But her son, who looked to be around the same age as Ryan, was always so full of life and happiness getting in and out of that car every day.

"I know. Cheesy. It's my favorite line from my favorite movie that nobody else has ever heard of. *It Came Upon a Midnight*

Clear. It's one of those made for TV Christmas specials. Mickey Rooney plays a wonderful grandfather and, at the end, his grandson says, 'Christmas is what you make of it.' The grandfather replies, 'Life is what you make of it.' And there you have it." She turned towards Thomas and smiled. "My life's philosophy in 30 seconds."

Thomas chuckled. "At least you have one. I mean it's good. It's really good. Much better than mine. Honestly, I don't think I can even share my philosophy in 30 seconds. I've never tried." Thomas could not believe he was even having this conversation in the rain. Just a few short weeks ago, he would have abruptly and efficiently ended this conversation – it was the kind of discussion he had always considered frivolous, pointless. As water dripped down his forehead, Thomas was struck by the irony. He would invest countless hours to create a business strategy on a page, but working out a philosophy for purpose in life, this was somehow not worth the investment?

"I'm Thomas." He held out his hand.

"Clara. Thank you, Thomas." Her voice trailed off softly as if reflecting on something that she didn't want to discuss.

"Sure thing. Thanks for what?"

"For listening to my philosophy." Clara sounded like this was a big deal.

"Oh, right. It's good. I mean that. And thank you for sharing it."

"What time is…" she glanced at her phone and abruptly turned towards her car. "Gotta run. See you around, Thomas."

He just stood there for what must have been more than a minute. His hair was wet, his shoulders were wet, even his shoes were starting to soak through. Normally this would have frustrated Thomas, but today he just stood there, thinking about everything and thinking about nothing.

The New Normal

As Thomas walked back to sister's apartment to get his car, he stepped in a puddle after puddle without even noticing. His mind was in high gear, piecing together a plan. Just an hour later, Thomas was sitting in the quietest corner of the local library with a stack of books and a notepad. He chuckled to himself, wondering why he hadn't thought of this plan earlier. With just a few phone calls and emails, Thomas has arranged for a former customer to buy the intellectual property of the company, the company that had been his baby. The price wasn't substantial – it was far below what Thomas knew the market could pay – but this customer would take care of all the details that had been consuming Thomas' days and nights. Thomas would be practically broke, his business would be gone forever, but this would buy him a little time. He hoped this little time would be enough. A very different smile was pasted across his face as he flipped through the small mountain of books and scribbled notes that were barely legible even for him. By early afternoon, the sun had reclaimed the sky, but Thomas hadn't even noticed. His stack of books consumed him. Such was the methodical and all-consuming way that Thomas had always approached his work. The day went by like a blink of an eye, and Thomas nearly missed pick-up time for Ryan.

Most of the large stack of library books now occupied the car's front seat as Thomas pulled in to the elementary school parking lot. Ryan was one of a handful of children still awaiting a ride home. His small face wore a troubled expression and he barely looked up as he climbed into the back seat.

"Hey buddy! The sun's out!" Thomas reminisced on his own school days, when he would be so surprised by the rapid lengthening of daylight hours. Even though it followed a predictable rhythm, the spring still had a magical feeling of new life and more of everything good.

Ryan didn't return his uncle's enthusiasm. Not today.

"What's up, bud? Lots of homework?"

"No. I did it already while I was waiting for you." The words were quiet, but Ryan's face and body practically shouted, *I don't really want to talk about it!*

Ryan rarely did his homework while waiting to be picked up. On most afternoons, he was too busy playing with his friends. Today was different. They drove in silence for a few minutes before Ryan looked up and asked, "Uncle Tommy, where are we going?"

"Exploring. You'll see." Thomas spoke slowly, deliberately building suspense. "You and me... we're going on an adventure together."

The boy's glum face brightened just a bit.

"Uncle Tommy, is it far away? I mean really far away?"

"It's not too far away buddy."

"Oh." Ryan sounded less than enthusiastic.

"We do have to drive a few more minutes, but we're almost there."

"Ok," came the disappointed reply. Thomas looked at his little nephew in the rear-view mirror and saw sorrow across the boy's face. Thomas was still on an emotional high from the progress he'd made in the library earlier and he hoped that an adventure would be just the thing to cheer Ryan up. They pulled into a small parking lot carved out of a dense forest. Ryan was slow to get out of the car.

How unlike him, thought Thomas. Without a word, they headed up a trail that would lead to an adventure neither could have expected. The ground was still a bit wet from that morning's rain, and the warm spring sun seemed to beckon life from the moist earth. They had been trekking silently for several minutes when Ryan softly sang, "This land is my land, this land is your land." Thomas looked over at his partner and their eyes connected. Without realizing it, Thomas had been humming this old folk song for the last few hundred yards. Now, they sang through the verses aloud together. Thomas remembered so many family vacations when he and Tiff would sing at the top of their lungs in their parent's old rusty station wagon. Tiff must have taught Ryan a few of those classics. That brought a smile to Thomas' face.

Their voices grew to a crescendo, "This land was made for you and me!"

"Is it real, uncle Tommy?"

"Is what real, buddy?"

"The song. The singing. Is it *really* real?"

"I think it is." Thomas wanted it to be *really* real. At this moment, on this day, deep in a peaceful forest, it seemed like the world could have been made just for the two of them.

Ryan's face had the look of amazement. "There's singing when Aslan makes the world – I mean Narnia. Remember? And all the talking animals? Was he singing that song to them? Was he singing 'This land is your land' to – um – what are their names? Polly and…" Ryan was deep in thought for few seconds searching for the boy's name, before moving on with the excitement of a child on the morning of his birthday, "Uncle Tommy, do you think this could be Narnia? Look!! That tree looks like a lamppost. I think we're in Narnia! Uncle Tommy this is so cool! I've never met a talking animal. I want to meet a talking animal."

The boy's enthusiasm was contagious. Thomas had to stop himself, as he almost blurted out something along the lines of, "Well, that's not actually possible." He had always had mixed feelings about feeding a child's belief in imaginary places and creatures. Something about the moment allowed Thomas to join Ryan's world. He crouched down, put his arm on the boy's shoulder, and pointed towards the lamppost tree. "That one, there?"

A nod was enough response to inspire Thomas to continue. "Ryan, let's explore deeper into the wood." Both adventurers were now breathing and treading quietly, knowing that something mysterious was up ahead. They left the well-worn hiking path in pursuit of something big, something grand, something unknown. A phrase Thomas had read and re-read earlier that day kept echoing in his mind. "We may ignore, but we can nowhere evade the presence of God. The world is crowded with Him. He walks everywhere incognito." C.S. Lewis, the brilliant imagination behind Narnia, had written this, but Ryan had said the same thing – albeit with different words – just that morning. "Aslan's always there."

As they hiked through thickets, around granite outcroppings, and paused to observe trees Ryan pointed out that looked like giant's utensils, Thomas ran through the day's mental and emotional journey. He had decided to write his "30 second philosophy of the purpose of life" and had poured over books that might provide clues to the approach others had taken with this same task. In many ways, it felt like an exercise he had conducted repeatedly throughout his life, only this time the question was different. In the past, he had searched for marketing, funding, selling, and hiring strategies. He always called it "Standing on the Shoulders of Giants," a phrase borrowed from his high school calculus teacher, whose passion for Isaac Newton translated into weekly quotes and anecdotes often related to *the father of the calculus.* Thomas laughed to himself. "The songs of a nation, indeed," he thought. How had Joseph put it just a few weeks ago? "Whose words do you let affect you?" Yeah, that's what Joseph said, or something like it anyway. Wow!

A profound thought washed over Thomas. He had always let philosophies and world-views affect him, even if it wasn't planned or intentional. As he had studied companies and business strategies, the philosophy of those he studied had been allowed influence on his entire life. Sure, he would ask questions about their approach, but the most common question was some form of, "Will that work in my business, in today's market?" He wanted their results, but not once had he asked if the business leaders he studied were the kind of person he wanted to become. An image of that high school calculus teacher popped into his mind. He could just imagine his teacher turning one of Thomas' famously sarcastic questions around. Thomas had once raised his hand in class and, when called on, had exclaimed, "This is great stuff! I can see so many practical applications." The teacher nodded and Thomas continued, "If we all become calculus teachers, we'll use this pretty much every single year." His classmates thought this was hilarious. The teacher did not. On another occasion, Thomas ever so politely inquired, "Do you want to become Isaac Newton when you grow up?" The room erupted with laughter and Thomas got to spend a little quality time in the principal's office. This was the question Thomas could now see being turned around. Why was it so clear now, while it had never even crossed his mind in the past? The answer was right there. What are you looking for?

Thomas retraced his hours at the library with this question as the filter. He had pulled dozens of books out of the biography section, looking for clues about creating clarity. Which biographies were the best to study? His filter had changed dramatically over the course of just a few hours. The first stack of biographies he brought to the table included business leaders, politicians, military leaders, inventors, sports stars, and a few random well-known historic figures. It was the last category that changed Thomas' filter. Martin Luther King, Jr. – what did he really know about MLK? Thomas skimmed a few chapter headings and was captivated by the quotes that started each chapter. He now had pages filled with quotes by Dr. King, but the one that had stopped him in his tracks was not by King. King had loved to read Plato and it was Plato's quote that leapt from the page. "Only those who do not seek power are qualified to hold it."

Standing in the rain earlier that morning, Thomas had made what he thought was a simple decision to write up a 30 second philosophy. He thought he would get on with his next business venture after completing this simple task. Now he knew that the journey might shake up everything. He was not looking for that. Or was he? He poured over that Martin Luther King book for over an hour, then returned every other book to the shelves and stood next to the "K's" to learn more about this legend. He grabbed a few more books about the civil rights legend and then noticed the word "Lewis" on a neighboring shelf. Carl Lewis. The great Olympic runner. Sports occupied a special place for Thomas. But then his glance landed on "C.S. Lewis". Not one or two books, but several. Who was the man behind the incredible stories Thomas had been reading with Ryan? He had walked back to his table with a stack of books about King and Lewis. The lives and words of these two men would occupy the next several hours and many of the books would end the day sitting in the BMW's passenger seat. Among the books was a notebook filled with ideas, quotes, and questions that Thomas would wrestle with for a long time.

"Uncle Tommy, look!" Ryan shouted as he pointed towards an impressive waterfall. He was running now and quickly separated himself from Thomas by a few dozen yards.

"Wait up, Ryan." Thomas jogged to catch up, just as Ryan reached a ledge next to the waterfall. He had hiked this mountain many times but didn't recall ever seeing this waterfall. They must have ventured further from the marked trails than Thomas realized. "Wow! It's amazing, isn't it?"

"Yeah. I want to climb down there." Ryan gestured towards a rock ledge about thirty feet below them. It looked like it was carved there for the sole purpose of being discovered and explored, like a throne for a woodland king.

"Sure. Let's do it!" Thomas was caught up in the adventure and replied without thinking about the time, the earlier rain, or what Tiff might say.

The loud, majestic waterfall towered above them to the left. To their immediate right, a rocky path welcomed the adventurers. It was steep, but offered plenty of roots, small trees, and rocks as a form of handrail for their descent. Occasionally, Ryan would reach for his uncle's hand to get through a difficult section, but they were making great progress.

"Whoa! Hold up." Thomas stopped abruptly as the path seemed to all but vanish. In front of them was a drop-off. To their left, the rock face was wet from an irregular splashing coming from the waterfall, as it ricocheted off the adjacent wall of granite. Thomas gripped Ryan's hand with his own left hand and placed his right hand firmly on the boy's shoulder. "It looks like the end of the road, buddy." Thomas and Ryan just looked in awe at the incredible grandeur and beauty created by the simple combination of water, gravity, and time.

"It's right there! It's right there! It's a throne. A rock throne. We have to get there. Come on, Uncle Tommy!" Ryan practically forgot how close he was to the ravine's edge and his whole body surged forward with anticipation. He was pointing to the rock ledge they had seen from above that had inspired this waterfall climb.

"I don't know, buddy." Thomas looked for another route, but nothing looked safe. In his mind, he could hear Tiff's cautious and oft-repeated motherly warnings, *"Don't be crazy. He's six. Try to remember that!"* Surely Tiff would hear about this, he thought, knowing that Ryan would be so excited to tell his mother every detail of this adventure. Thomas also realized that his sister was fully aware of Ryan's gift of making every adventure sound more dangerous than it had been. This might work to their advantage. Yes, thought Thomas. He could picture Tiff listening to Ryan recreating the whole adventure and Tiff nodding with that great look of awe she used so well to let her little guy know she was right there with him. Tiff would presume that the story had been exaggerated and Thomas wouldn't be in any trouble. The matter was settled. They would find a way to get to that throne. Besides, Thomas was so happy to see that whatever had been troubling Ryan earlier now seemed to be forgotten.

"There must be a secret passage. We'll have to go back up and find it. Remember, it's not always easy to spot secret passages, and you've got the best eyes." As he heard his uncle's words, Ryan was absolutely beaming. Thomas still held onto the boy firmly as they turned to go back up the path. Ryan suddenly lunged forward.

"Right there! Look! That's it!"

"Hold on, buddy. We have to stick together for this part of the journey. What do you see?" Thomas quickly positioned his body between Ryan and the drop-off, starting to feel a bit nervous about this whole scenario. "What? Where?"

Ryan clutched his uncle's waist, leaned out towards the open chasm, and stared. In a near whisper, he slowly explained, "The secret passage. I found it."

Thomas shook his head in disbelief. Right there, just a few feet below them, was a narrow rock ledge that lead straight to the throne. Only one word could describe what he saw. "Wow!"

"Awesome, right Uncle Tommy? You go down first. But don't let me go." Ryan's face said it all. They were conquering a great opponent, doing the impossible, taking on Goliath, and Ryan was simultaneously petrified and ready to go. Thomas calculated his first few steps and searched for a good hand grip. He would lower himself down and, for the initial drop, all his weight would be supported by one hand. It looked easy enough until his feet were dangling beneath him. Ryan kept a firm grip on Thomas' right hand while the left was supporting his entire body. Knees scraped against the rock face and Thomas breathed quite loudly. His left foot stretched down for something solid. Nothing. After adjusting his left arm angle, both feet made it to the ledge. "That got the blood flowing," he thought to himself, as he helped Ryan lower his body down to the ledge. Thankfully, the ledge was even wider than it looked from above. They worked their way towards the throne and were soon seated together on this massive rock bench. While the waterfall had looked impressive before, their view from this natural throne was breathtaking.

There they sat, conquerors, kings, knights, explorers. Triumphant! Ryan's face said it all. But then, suddenly, his face transformed into disbelief, even awe. Ryan leaned back in the throne, and manipulated the angle of his head. He tilted to the left, to the right, now forward and to the left, now back.

"Whoa! How...? Awesome!" Amazement resonated in the boy's voice. Thomas just looked at him, not wanting to interrupt the moment. "To see the world through the eyes of a six-year-old, if only for a moment," Thomas thought, "what a gift!" But then he saw it, too. The ledge, their secret passage, had disappeared. Thomas froze and felt sick in his stomach. He felt his heart begin to race and searched for another way to return from this rock ledge. He found nothing. How was this possible?

"This is so awesome, Uncle Tommy!" Ryan's voice interrupted Thomas' short, but vivid, nightmare. "How does it do that?"

"Do what, Ryan?"

"Look! It's there and it's not. The secret passage."

Thomas let his gaze follow Ryan's and then he understood. The rock ledge path was right there. Incredible. When looking from a certain angle, it would completely blend into the surrounding rock. Thomas decided not to explain the optical illusion to Ryan just yet. They could discuss it later, perhaps another day. Let it remain a mystery for now. It certainly felt mysterious. Soon enough, the two adventurers would have something more pressing than an optical illusion to consume their thoughts.

After they stared for what seemed like many minutes, captivated by the disappearing and reappearing secret path, Thomas broke the silence. "Are you ready for the journey back across the ledge?"

"What ledge?" Ryan kidded with his uncle. "I don't see any path!"

Thomas smiled, knowing that the boy had picked up some of his humor from his uncle. Then he took the first step onto the ledge. Within a few steps, both climbers were completely silent, focusing all their attention on each movement. It seemed more precarious on the return trip. They locked arms and cautiously continued. "Make sure you have a good grip with your free hand, buddy." Thomas didn't look down as he said these words. He was focused on his own grip.

They were only a few feet away from safety when Thomas started to panic. There was nothing to hold on to here. He looked again, straining his eyes and trying to recall this section from their first crossing. Had he really just walked on this narrow rock ledge, much like a tight-rope walker, but with a solid rock face on one side? He only now realized that sweat was dripping off his brow. His hands were sweaty, too, so he tightened his grip on his six-year-old nephew. This boy meant so much to him. When Thomas looked down, his reaction was sudden and unexpected. His body lurched, almost instinctively, away from the open ravine but back toward the solid rock. The movement was too abrupt, too forceful. His right shoulder and chest caromed off the rock and he reached out with his right hand for something, anything, to stop his deflected momentum from casting him into the ravine. Nothing. He flailed again, extending his arm as his right foot was pulled off the ledge. There was nothing to grab on to. He made one last desperate reach and his right thumb and pointer grasped something. The two fingers locked and held fast, jarring Thomas' whole body, but keeping him from free-falling down into the ravine. His right leg was dangling below the ledge, his left foot still supported some weight, and Ryan's right arm was clenched tightly by Thomas' left hand. Ryan said nothing, but his eyes were locked on his uncle. Thomas couldn't even look at the boy. His energy was consumed in the attempt to bring his right leg back up to the ledge. By this point, his right middle and ring fingers had joined the pointer and thumb in clasping around the small, but solid, root of an unknown tree protruding ever so slightly above the secret passage.

"Ryan, stay right there. Just hold on. Do you have a good grip with your other hand?"

Ryan just nodded in response and squeezed Thomas' left hand even harder.

The angle was too much for Thomas and he could feel the fingers on his right hand beginning to get numb, but he just squeezed them together harder. Were they touching? He couldn't tell, as the only feeling they seemed to register was a cramping sensation in that hand and forearm. With every ounce of strength, he got the toes of his right foot onto the ledge, but they slipped off. There was still some moisture on the ledge from the rain earlier that day. The force on his right arm was almost unbearable, but he had to bear it. His left leg was bent further than he thought possible, and his muscles quivered under the pressure. He had to make it on this next attempt. He was convinced that his right arm, left leg, or both would give way if he slipped one more time. Thomas breathed very deeply, deliberately, giving his muscles a few seconds to regain some strength for another attempt. His mind raced, bombarded with thoughts of the worst. He imagined the news story, "Local Woman loses Husband, then Son and Brother." He pictured Tiff's face, then his dead brother-in-law's. Now, Thomas, NOW! It seemed almost as if his deceased brother-in-law was shouting to him in a dream. Thomas summoned every last ounce of strength, thrusting his right foot away, up, and then back towards the ledge. His toes cleared the ledge and caught just a bit of solid ground. Was it enough this time? Pain pulsed through his right arm, but he ignored it. His pushed up with his left leg just as he felt the fingers on his right hand letting go. No! The right foot didn't have enough grip to hold his weight. He felt a warm breeze and it seemed like two hands pushed his body up and forward. Nearly overcome with exhaustion, Thomas found himself standing on the ledge. His right hand still gripped the root and his muscles pulsated. Thomas took in a few rapid breaths, realizing that he had stopped breathing for a few moments as he made this desperate attempt to regain his footing. He reached down to Ryan and, within a few seconds, the uncle and his nephew stood, side-by-side, on solid ground.

"Ryan, are you okay? I'm so sorry!" Thomas put his hands to his face and then picked the boy up and squeezed him like he would never let go. "We made it!"

"Uncle Tommy…" The boy hesitated and looked out into the ravine. The sound of the waterfall filled the canyon, although Thomas had completely shut out its noise just a few moments ago. Ryan continued, "Of course we made it."

"Yeah, of course." Thomas didn't feel like it was an of course!

Ryan looked at his uncle and his statement would keep Thomas awake that night, "We didn't finish the books yet. Daddy wants us to finish the books."

Thomas couldn't coax his mouth or vocal cords to respond. He opened his mouth, but no words came. Instead, a single large tear dropped from one eye and he gave his nephew an even tighter bear hug while his head slowly nodded up and down.

Minutes seemed to pass before they turned to hike back to the car. Thomas kept turning the experience over and over in his mind, trying to come to grips with what had happened, why it had happened, and what had all too nearly happened. On the long drive back to Tiff's house, Ryan was back to his talkative self, and was about to let Thomas deeper into his world.

Why, Uncle Tommy, Why?

"Uncle Tommy, why do you think the secret passage disappeared like that? Is it magic? It has to be magic. Secret passages are always magic." Ryan was so excited as the BMW headed back to his mom's apartment. Thomas was half listening and half planning, as he wrestled with the best approach for the upcoming conversation with his sister. "Uncle Tommy, why did your foot slip? Uncle Tommy, I was wondering…" Ryan looked like he was nibbling on the left side of his lower lip. Thomas remembered the boy's mother doing this when she was about the Ryan's age. It often meant she was figuring out something serious.

"What, buddy?" He looked at the little guy in the rearview mirror and could see that his nephew was really struggling with something. "What were you wondering?"

Ryan was quiet for a few moments before quietly and deliberately asking, "Why do bad things happen?" He stared down at his shoes, with a mix of relief at asking the question and sorrow for not wanting to have the discussion. It was a question and discussion that Ryan had been working through on his own for a while now.

Thomas wasn't ready for this question. It reminded him of one of those perfect black and white TV programs his parents had always liked. The kid asks a good question and the parents seem to have the perfect concise answer ready just in time. They share their incredible wisdom, the child understands, repeats the wisdom, and the show concludes with its upbeat theme song. Since Thomas was not ready with a wise answer, he decided to buy some time. "What do you mean, Ryan?" As soon as the words left his mouth, he wished he could take them back. This might buy some time, but it also might make the question much more complicated than Thomas wanted.

"Well, Jamey – he's a boy in my class – he forgot to…" Ryan spoke rapid-fire and shared a long series of stories about some troubles with his friends at school recently. Thomas breathed a sigh of relief, thinking he may have avoided the tough question for today, but he would soon find out that he was wrong. Very wrong.

While Ryan spoke, Thomas was thinking about the conversation that he thought he had avoided – Ryan's father, Paul. The two had yet to really discuss what Thomas wished no six-year-old, especially his only nephew, would ever have to experience. Paul had been a great dad, when he was around. Thomas and Paul were friends from college, and that was how Paul and Tiff had met. Even though Thomas was always the protective older brother, he let his guard down when Tiff started to show interest in Paul. It was over the summer when Paul and Thomas had just finished their junior year of college and had decided to get an apartment in town so they could start a small enterprise together. It was a great partnership. Paul was patient, methodical, and great with software. Thomas filled in the rest of the picture with his budding business skills. He was a salesman that instinctively seemed to know how to price and position their services, and got enough business over that summer that the two almost didn't return to college for their senior year. Paul had held firm with his decision that finishing college was a must. After much passionate debate, Thomas had given in and they returned to school two weeks after the fall semester had started. They continued to work diligently at growing their small business and neither had to attend a single interview through senior year. Their "jobs" were lined up. Or so it seemed.

Just a few months before graduation, Paul shared the news. It was received like a ton of bricks. He was going to be training for deployment. Joining the military had been a no-brainer for Paul. Several generations in his family had served. Paul's family was in that no-man's area financially, where they could certainly not afford college, but were too "well-off" to get much financial aid. Paul signed up and never looked back. The day that he signed the original commitment, deployment seemed like something that wouldn't happen again for decades, if ever. But now, with just a few months left before graduation and a growing business that needed his full attention and talents, deployment was the word that – try as he did – he just couldn't get used to saying. There was no official date… yet. The announcement simply described training in preparation for possible deployment. Maybe the day would never come, but somehow Paul knew that this was just wishful thinking. Besides, he had always known that if he were asked to fight for his country, to sacrifice for the cause of liberty, he would be willing.

By this time, Paul and Tiff had begun dating and seemed to have a connection that others would notice. So often they would hear the comments: "You're so good together!" "What a great couple!" "Are you two married?" "When's the big day?" They were certainly far from perfect as a couple, but they did seem to complete each other quite well. Tiff always laughed at Paul's jokes. His sense of humor wasn't for everyone, but she just loved the depth and thoughtfulness of his conversations. Paul was always asking questions that spoke volumes. People knew he was thinking of them and trying to understand their point of view by the way he listened, reflected, and inquired. A deeply authentic and often used phrase Tiff had grown to love was, "I appreciate that perspective. What shaped your thinking here?" Paul's curiosity was almost child-like. Not childish, but child-*like*. He really cared about ideas and really wanted to know what others thought.

They weren't engaged – yet – and had not even discussed marriage. However, to all that knew the couple well, marriage was a foregone conclusion. It was only a matter of when. After the announcement that Paul would be trained for possible deployment, the next few years went by like a whirlwind. Tiff and Paul were married. Paul had to spend a considerable amount of time in military training, and the fledgling company that Paul and Thomas had started was put on hold. Thomas channeled his energy and the lessons into another venture, while any free time Paul had was dedicated to wedding plans, buying and fixing up a small starter home, and volunteering at a local soup kitchen. Thomas admired Paul's servant heart, but never really got involved with that.

When Tiff announced that they were pregnant with Ryan, Thomas was so tied up in his work that he just texted her a quick "Congratulations!" from one of many airports. By this point, Paul had been sent on several overseas missions. For military purposes, he couldn't share much about his trips and his demeanor was changing more than Tiff imagined possible. Paul's patience, authenticity, and deep concern for others was fading. He rarely showed up at the soup kitchen, opting instead to hang out with some buddies at a local bar. When Tiff asked about work, or what was on his mind, Paul usually changed the subject or practically ignored the question. Tiff decided that this was a part of his life that she might best leave alone. As baby Ryan turned into toddler Ryan, explorer Ryan, and then kindergartener and first-grader Ryan, Paul oscillated between the best dad and a distant father. He would be on for a few days and then off for a week or more. During the "off" times, Ryan tried to connect with his dad is so many ways, but eventually learned to entertain himself and let his daddy come around when he chose to. Sometimes Tiff could tell that this bothered Paul. Other times, it looked like Paul appreciated the space.

It was a tour of duty just after Ryan's fifth birthday that accelerated Paul's transformation. Training was more intense that Tiff remembered it being. Paul would duck out of the house just after Ryan's bedtime several nights a week to meet up with friends in town to "grab a beer and let off some steam." Tiff didn't like this direction, but Paul had told her many times that she just "couldn't understand." She wanted to. She at least wanted the chance to try to understand. How could she be there for her husband, for her little boy's father? Tiff, who always knew what to say, was at a loss for words. What did Paul need from her now?

Then he was gone. With very little notice, Paul was deployed. They were hugging goodbye with tears flowing freely. Ryan loved his daddy so much. Tiff didn't want to let the embrace to end. When Paul finally turned and walked away, Ryan paused briefly, and then ran after his daddy and jumped up on Paul. The little guy was no longer trying to fight back his tears. "I love you, Daddy! I love you! I love you! I love you!"

"Me too, Ryan. I love you so much! I'm sorry. Daddy will be back soon, promise!" Paul almost choked on the words as they tumbled out of his mouth. Of course, he would be back soon, but not soon from a five-year-old's perspective. Not soon for his lovely wife who spent about half their marriage living like a single mom. Paul hugged Ryan so tightly, kissed him on the cheek, and then he was gone.

This tour felt different from the very beginning. Tiff didn't like it and, to no avail, had tried several times to initiate a conversation about it with Paul. She wanted to tell him how proud she was that he served his country, that he was willing to make such a sacrifice. She also wanted to tell him that maybe it was time to just be a husband and father. She never had that chance.

Days turned into weeks and weeks turned into months. Tiff and Ryan sent several letters every week, each one full of artwork and experiences that Ryan wished so desperately to share with his father. They got to talk on the phone every now and again, but Paul's mission and state of mind were not conducive to consistent communication. When they did talk, however, Paul sounded very different. It was a good different. A very good different. He sounded like the old Paul, the one Tiff had laughed with so easily just a few years ago. The Paul that played with baby Ryan without letting anything else interrupt. Tiff could tell that this mission was a tough one for Paul, but somehow, he was winning. He was dreaming again, sharing ideas for things they'd do in the future. It was something they did all the time in the first few years of their marriage, but this had vanished as Paul's outlook had slipped. Were Tiff and Ryan going to get the old Paul back? Would this last? Tiff often found herself sitting at the kitchen table late into the night, dreaming of the life that she was so sure they would share when Paul's mission was over. Dreaming of family dinners, playing games in the yard, taking walks, bike rides, singing songs together, road trips, trips to the beach. She realized that Paul was not the only one who had stopped dreaming somewhere along the way. It felt good, refreshing, invigorating, to think of what could be.

Just a few days after Christmas, Tiff read the message. Paul was coming home. He'd be stateside in a few weeks, with a brief stop at a military base by the coast. Then, he'd be home. When her phone rang, Tiff almost dropped it, she was so excited. "I'm coming home!" Paul repeated the sentence quietly several times, as if in disbelief. "We're ready for you, sweetheart!" Tiff's radiant smile was pasted across her face. They chatted excitedly for a few minutes about the details of the return home before Paul said, "It will be different, hon. I realized a few things. Us. Our family. There's good in the world and bad, and plenty in between. But what matters most? I've been thinking about that a lot lately. What matters most? You, Tiff. And Ryan. Us. Our family. It's one of the most important things in all of life. I'm so sorry, I know I haven't been there enough. I've been messing one of the most important things up. The fighting, the sadness, the bad in the world... it got to me. No, I let it get to me. I let it. Even the soup kitchen. I stopped helping out there. That was so important. I had friends there, they would smile and talk with me every time I was there. They'd tell me about their day and ask about mine. What matters most, Tiff? Loving and being loved."

Tiff's smile had only grown bigger as he talked. Tears of joy streamed down her face. It seemed like a dream until she felt a tug on her hand. "What's wrong, Mommy?" Ryan was still in his pajamas and observed her tears with a deep look of concern.

"It's Paul – It's Daddy! Daddy's coming home!" She handed the phone to Ryan and his face absolutely lit up.

"Daddy!" Ryan's whole body was literally bouncing up and down. Ryan told his father about everything that happened over Christmas, and that he had a lot of days off from school. "Maybe four or twelve. How many days was it, Mommy?"

After the phone call, Ryan was walking on air for the rest of Christmas vacation week. He kept asking, "Mom, is it today? When is Daddy going to get here? In the morning?" Tiff kept trying to explain that it was still a few weeks away, but both mother and son wished the day would arrive already.

When that day did finally arrive, Tiff and Ryan were just finishing dinner together when the door knob turned. Ryan practically jumped out of and over his chair in one swift movement. As Paul opened the door, it almost took the sprinting Ryan down. The two embraced in the best bear hug Ryan could remember. That evening and the next few weeks were incredible. Everything between Tiff and Paul felt like it had when they were just married. Tiff was thrilled to have this Paul back home. They talked, dreamed, and Paul spent more time with Ryan than ever. Tiff's two boys, one a smaller version of the other, were practically inseparable. She didn't want to pinch herself for fear that she might wake up. But wake up – and too abruptly – she would.

The Knock no Mother Should Answer

It was just a few weeks after Paul's return and Tiff pulled her car in the driveway. Ryan was playing at a friend's house. She rummaged through the refrigerator, trying to figure out what to make for dinner. She expected Paul to arrive back home any minute when she heard a knock at the door. Tiff closed the refrigerator and walked to the front door. Two state police officers solemnly asked to enter the house. The one who did most of the talking seemed barely able to look her in the eyes. After identifying themselves, the officer confirmed Tiff's full name and then asked her to confirm her marriage status to Paul, his full name, and several other details. Tiff was completely caught off guard. "What is this about? Is something wrong?"

The officer's voice was quiet and quivered ever so slightly. "I have been asked to inform you that there was a car accident. Your husband has been reported dead on impact." Tiff could feel nothing as these words slammed into her. Her face dropped and her gaze locked on the floor tiles. Everything went blurry. Her mouth hung open, as her entire face felt numb. The officer was still explaining something, but nothing seemed to register. He body was shaking uncontrollably as she responded with a series of barely discernable sounds "Mmm Huh… Ohhh… No… No…"

Tiff didn't remember showing the officers to the door and had no idea how much time had gone by when she jolted up from a collapsed sobbing position on the kitchen floor. Ryan! She had to pick him up. She grabbed her cell phone and glanced at the time. Oh no! She was late. Scrolling through the messages, she saw a text message saying Ryan was on his way home. His friend's mother would be there in a few minutes to drop him off. Tiff sank back into a kitchen chair, her body completely overwhelmed and

43

trembling with sickly rhythm. She normally had all the answers to help her friends through tough situations, but right now she had nothing. Disbelief seemed the only acceptable route. But the officer's words replayed in her mind again and again. The officer had all the details – Paul's car, his wallet with license, Paul's description – it was her Paul. It was Ryan's daddy. They just got him back. Why would this happen to her little family? She knew it couldn't be real, but she knew it was. Ryan would walk in the door within minutes. Their little boy. Her little boy. Tiff's mind raced through images like a master film-maker, bringing up memories that they would cherish forever and future pinnacle moments without a daddy. Her breathing became very rapid. Now she was standing, pacing very rapidly around the house with blood angrily pumping through every muscle in her being. She clenched and unclenched her fists, shook her arms out, paused to stare at the wall and try to get her breathing and racing heart under some semblance of control. Ryan... Ryan! She had to be composed for Ryan. He already was the focal point of her life, and now, especially now, she needed to be strong for him. She did not have a plan. She had no idea what to say to her little boy. Is there any way to be prepared for this? A mother shouldn't have to give her child this kind of news. She would hug Ryan. That's all she could think to do.

"Mommy!!! You're not even going to believe what I look like. Mommy!!! Mommy? Are you hiding?" Ryan's voice was so full of excitement.

"I'm here, honey." Tiff's voice came out in a whisper, just loud enough for Ryan to locate her.

"Close your eyes, Mommy!" She was thankful to be asked to close her eyes. She covered her face with her hands, wiping tears as little running feet approached her. "Look, Mommy, look! You can look now, Mommy!!" She felt his hands, one on her leg and the other pulling on her hand. "Open your eyes, Mommy! See?

See? I'm a lion!" Tiff's face must have been a complete mess as she opened her eyes to see the painted face of her priceless little boy. He was a lion, alright. Tiff's tears mixed with a big smile. It was a smile full of both joy and sadness. "Isn't it great, Mommy? Raaahhhrrrrr! But I'm a good lion… a nice and friendly lion."

The next few weeks were a blur, with time going by in an alternating, yet unpredictable pattern of fast and slow speeds. A day might seem like the blink of an eye, while another moment seemed to last for several days.

Life doesn't Wait

A job? Thomas wasn't sure he heard correctly. He was on the phone with the dean of a local college and it sounded like they were offering him not one, but two jobs. After diving into the world of business ownership, J-O-B had become a word that Thomas thought he would create for others. For quite some time now, he had not really considered himself eligible for one of these "job" things.

"Tell me more," was all he could think to respond. It was a phrase he had mastered during countless sales conversations throughout his business career. The dean obliged to fill Thomas in on the college administration's search for a baseball coach as well as their interest in exploring an instructor to help them build an entrepreneurship track. The baseball coach was the immediate need and apparently Thomas still had some credibility as a baseball player from his high school and college career. A member of the college's board had put his name in the hat, saying Thomas just might be the right man to shape the character of these young athletes and to build the program. The second job, testing the waters by offering a few courses in entrepreneurship, was a separate item for that board meeting, but apparently the same board member had once again brought up Thomas' name and track record.

"Interesting..." and "I certainly appreciate being considered..." were two of the phrases Thomas heard himself say, in an effort to keep the dean speaking while he tried to put this scenario in perspective. Baseball and starting a business were two of his favorite topics. In light of his current unusual business circumstances, Thomas would actually have the time to do both, but having a boss... that concept wasn't something Thomas was sure he was ready for.

"Yes, I would love to come to campus to continue the conversation." He could hardly believe that he had said this, and the date of their formal interview was established. An interview!

Thomas had scheduled so many, but felt very uneasy being on the other side of the table.

Of course, he knew that he would turn down any potential offer. Even though he had a strange sense of peace about this coincidental offer to be involved in two passions simultaneously, Thomas was sure that he was not a teacher, coach, or even very employable, for that matter. He had his own ways of doing things, had never even tried to fit in to someone else's organizational structure, and certainly didn't see how his independent spirit would fit in a structured college setting with course outlines, curriculum, and who-knows-what-else involved. This was decided. He would politely decline.

About an hour after the interviews, Thomas found himself standing in front of the same park bench where he had met the mysterious Joseph so many weeks ago. He was throwing rocks into the water and talking to himself. A few passersby gave him puzzled looks. "Talk quietly," he said to himself. "Stop moving your lips," he muttered, a bit too loudly. A woman with two small dogs scurried away from him, glancing up with an expression that let Thomas know that she had hear this last phrase. "Sorry. Sorry. I was just talking to myself... I wasn't talking to you." He realized that there wasn't much he could say to the woman that might straighten this out. She hurried along, apparently not wanting to participate in any explanation.

He continued the conversation with himself in silence for a few minutes, throwing stone after stone into the river, before blurting out, "A job. Me. I have a job. No, two jobs." He nodded and forced a small smile in the direction of the couple standing a few feet away from him. They turned and walked away. Thomas kept nodding. I guess I do, he thought. He still wasn't sure how the dean had convinced him to say yes to both positions. He went to the interview – it was still hard to even say this word – with the clear resolution that he would not take either job. He couldn't. It was time for him to get back in the game, not take on a job or two. But now he was committed for a full school year. He would be the baseball coach, trying to turn around a flailing program, teach three courses on entrepreneurship, and head up the project of evaluating a new minor in entrepreneurship. What did he know about any of these jobs? Nothing. The strangest thing about this predicament was the sense of peace that had accompanied the decision.

Thomas felt an excitement that was familiar in some ways, yet starkly different. Many times, he had been full of this type of excitement when starting a business venture, growing a product line, building a customer base, or launching a marketing campaign. This time was different. It was a paradoxical sense of peace combined with uncertainty. He dealt well with uncertainty, but this uncertainty was more profound. It seemed that virtually every aspect of the new venture was concealed from his view. In business, he was generally able to create clarity around an end result, clarity to what he was chasing. In this new "job", he didn't even know where to start, let alone where he wanted to take any of the three roles. The peace that accompanied the excitement was the hardest for Thomas to try to explain to himself – but he kept trying, as if it needed a logical explanation.

His thoughts went back to a conversation with Paul in their few hours together just days before the accident. They had discussed "paradigm-shifts" – moments, experiences, ideas, perspectives, quotes, relationships – that are somehow able to change the way we look at, or lead, our lives. It had started out as a walk down memory lane, with the friends going back and forth with stories about teachers, coaches, girls, and other memorable moments that had left a profound mark. They laughed at how often moments that may have seemed insignificant turned out to be the big things, the most important lessons. They also reminisced at how many of their parents' repeated expressions contained wisdom that, years later, they would act as if they had uncovered on their own. The moment that stood out most came at the end of the conversation. Thomas had planned to pursue it further, but that would not happen. Paul had raised the stakes. He had casually asked, "If you could give your younger self just a few words of advice, maybe a motto to live by, what would it be?" They went back and forth on this for a few minutes, with words like: Live! Dream! Dare! Always try your hardest! Always have a great attitude!

"Carpe Diem! Seize the Day!" Paul whispered intensely, as he climbed onto a chair, reenacting a famous scene from *Dead Poets Society*.

They both laughed and then Paul said it. "It all changed for me with two words." This brought them back to the beginning of the conversation. Thomas had asked Paul to explain the deep change in him since his return from military service.

"Two words?" Thomas waited for his friend to continue. The silence seemed to last, and Thomas reflected on the way Paul had come back home with a different presence. Little things didn't get to him. He got along with people better and seemed to appreciate every aspect of life much more. Over these few weeks, Paul certainly still had his opinions, perhaps with even more conviction that ever before. What stood out the most was the way he communicated those opinions, offering a deep respect for those around him. They might disagree on an idea, but people could tell that Paul genuinely cared about them as people.

"Yes, just two words. Two words are what changed, and the same two words would be the guidance that I would share with my younger self. *I pray.* Simple. Two words. *I pray.*"

"Hmmmm. Yeah." Thomas acknowledged Paul and wondered if there was more that his friend could share. The two words were certainly simple, but there must be a more complete explanation.

His friend continued: "Each and every day, I find a few minutes of complete silence to spend in prayer." He paused and took a few deep breaths. "Every day. Every single day. I missed a few days when I was getting into the habit, but now I won't. It changes everything."

Thomas wanted to understand. "Like meditation?" He had several coaches and friends in business who recommended meditation over the years.

"Not sure." Paul shook his head, but seemed to know that his wife's big brother wanted a better explanation. "I sit or kneel for ten minutes or so. Occasionally shorter, but sometimes much longer. I pick things I am thankful for and talk to God silently about them, just saying thanks. Then I usually talk about the choices I've been making – maybe that day, the day before, or over the last few days – and say sorry about the choices that weren't the best. Sometimes just one of those topics will take up all the time I have. Other times, I tell God – or I guess pray – about something I am trying to figure out... like a disagreement I have with Tiff, or how to help Ryan learn to be responsible. I just quietly talk to God about some of these things and ask Him what He thinks I should do." Paul's eyes and body language said it all. Just explaining this experience flooded his whole body with a sense of calm.

"Wow!" was all Thomas said in response. He wasn't sure that he was one to take on "I pray" as a new daily habit, but he could absolutely see the impact it had on his brother-in-law. Thomas wanted – no he *needed* – more of this calming presence in his life.

There was so much more to discuss, so many questions Thomas wanted to ask. Did the praying experience always feel the same? Did Paul hear anything in response? Was it just like talking to yourself? Did Paul's prayerful moments ever feel childish? How could you tell if you were just imagining the conversation? Did it matter? Were there any other things Paul would discuss in these prayer sessions.

Thomas did not get to inquire further. Paul's phone rang, and Thomas heard him say, "Yeah, I'm heading home... love you, too."

Both men said they would continue the conversation another day, completely unaware that they would not get that chance.

As they parted company, Paul had put his arm on his friend's shoulder, looked squarely into his eyes and said, "Thomas, that's it. That's what I'd tell my younger self: 'When I pray, everything else makes sense.'"

They Call Me Coach

A few days after Thomas had somehow verbally accepted the job offer, he found himself walking across the college campus towards the baseball field. He was deep in thought, not just asking, but pursuing a very different question. When he told Tiff about his new jobs, she had just smiled warmly and remained silent. He told her about the decision from every angle for what must have been close to an hour before he finally asked her, "Ok, Tiff, what's with that big smile? You know something I don't?"

The wisdom and simplicity of her response just floored him. "He's always there."

"What?" Thomas asked, to buy himself time to think of a good response. A strange sense of continuity, of connectedness, washed over his whole body. He found himself just repeating his sister's words quietly, "He's always there. He's always there." Then the context came to him. "That's right, Aslan is always there! Ryan told you?"

"Yes, big brother, he did. He told me that you read the books and then he teaches you about the story. Ryan told me, 'Uncle Tommy needs me to help him understand Narnia. Adults don't get to go to Narnia, so they need kids to tell them about it.'" Her smile only grew larger as she moved closer to hug her brother. "Thank you!" she whispered. "You'll never know how much this has meant to Ryan... or to me."

So much had changed in just a few months. Thomas used to think he had a significant store of knowledge about the way the world worked, but now he wasn't so sure. The questions that Thomas now pursued came in many forms. At the core, it could be as simple as "What is the point?" The questions had many angles, but they all established meaning, purpose, a sense of why. "What is the real mission of a coach / teacher / uncle?" One version of the question he now pondered while walking to the baseball field: "How does all of this fit together perfectly?" All the difficulties, Paul's death, Thomas' business collapse, meeting Joseph, reading the books with Ryan, getting these seemingly unrelated, yet somehow overlapping jobs – they all seemed to be working together, and even in a positive direction. With this line of questions, came an assumption that Thomas might not have been willing to make just a few months prior. That assumption: life has a deeper purpose and that purpose runs much deeper than simply doing what you want or getting what you want. More than that, the purpose might often be in opposition to what you wanted. This had to fit into his roles of coach, teacher, uncle.

The baseball field was worse than a mess. Everything looked neglected. Equipment was in random places, parts of the infield dirt were overgrown, the pitcher's mound had two deep ruts where the pitcher's feet push off and land on every pitch. The batter's boxes had similar ruts, and the outfield fence was damaged in several places. As Thomas built one of his classic to-do lists, a strange idea came to him. It might not have been a strange idea for most people, but it was certainly not a typical idea for Thomas. He knew it was time to get to work, but the idea that gripped him came from that last conversation with Paul. "I pray and everything else makes sense." Thomas thought that he would take all of his "stuff" – his series of purpose questions, his rapidly growing to-do lists, and his new jobs – to prayer. Sure, he had family members and friends through the years that would say things like, "We're praying for you" and "I prayed about it," but he didn't really understand what this meant. He also had some of those well-rehearsed, sometimes poetic, prayers that the family would say on occasion. Today he would give his friend Paul's approach a more serious attempt. Sure, he had given it a few half-hearted attempts after their conversation, but now he would dive it and see for himself. If this was the sole advice Paul would give to his younger self, if this is what had helped

Paul make some significant changes in his life, Thomas could at least try it out.

He finished making his list at the field and then walked across the college campus to the small campus chapel. Would it be open? Would there be people inside? What does one say to people in a chapel in the middle of the afternoon? If a student, baseball player, or fellow teacher saw him, would they think he was one of "those" religious people? Thomas had entered so many board rooms, met with business executives across the country, yet today he was nervous about bumping into someone praying in a chapel. The door was open, and Thomas was relieved to find the chapel quiet, dimly lit, and empty. He sat down in the back corner, a familiar place from his occasional visits to church over the last few years. For a minute or two, Thomas just sat there, letting himself relax and just be in this beautiful space. His mind didn't remain quiet for long. He started thinking about all the stuff that came with the new jobs. Sure, he had played baseball, and played it well, even into college. But coaching a team and trying to build a program, that was a completely different challenge. They had no budget to speak of, for equipment, travel, uniforms, anything. After seeing the state of the field and the equipment, he wondered what kind of players to expect. On top of the college baseball team, he would be running a summer baseball camp for local kids, ages five through eighteen. What had he signed up for? Thomas found himself reaching into his pocket and taking out his cell phone to make a few notes and add items to the to-do list.

"What are you doing?" he thought to himself. This is supposed to be time for prayer. He put the phone on silent and back into his pocket. What had Paul said? He remembered there were three categories that Paul mentioned. Things he was thankful for was the first one. Thomas decided to start there. He closed his eyes and tried to get started. "I am thankful for…" he thought quietly "Ryan and Tiff." His eyes remained closed and a big smile formed across his face. He pictured so many of the things they had done together over the last few months. Hiking, baseball, barbecues, pizza, making up stories, reading. "I am thankful for reading, especially for those Narnia books." He thought of all the things Ryan remembered from the books and how he had so frequently made Thomas go back to reread a section. The little guy might not always seem like he was paying attention, but these stories, these characters, were really having an effect on him. "I am thankful for the imagination of the man who wrote those books!" Thomas was doing this prayer thing, at least to a degree. It felt very mechanistic to come back to "I am thankful for..." but he realized that when he picked one thing or one relationship and let his thoughts run with that one thing, he felt like he was actually sharing that memory with a close friend. It was a feeling that he longed for, a feeling he did not want to end.

The chapel door opened. Thomas suddenly felt self-conscious, opened his eyes and adjusted his posture to look like a man with everything under control. He tried not to look over to see who had entered, but found his eyes drawn towards the closing door. In the dim light, he could make out the shape of a large man walking slowly into the chapel. The shape of the man looked familiar. Could it be?

"Joseph!" Thomas realized that his voice was rather loud for this quiet, peaceful place, but he was pleased to see the familiar man walking towards him. "Joseph," he repeated, much softer, "we met a few months ago by the river. It's..."

"Thomas!" the man interrupted in his deep baritone. "Thomas! It is wonderful to see you, especially here." The richness and warmth of Joseph's voice was exactly what Thomas had struggled to describe to Tiff. The quality said more than the words alone could. "Tell me, Thomas, how goes your journey?"

Thomas proceeded to fill his friend in on the highlights of the last few months. He overflowed in sharing with Joseph everything about his most recent experiences, even the doubts and excitement. This was not typical of Thomas. He told Joseph about his new jobs and the initial resistance to taking them on.

"Is that what brings you here, into this chapel?" Joseph asked.

"Yes. Well, no, not entirely." Thomas wanted to tell his friend of the commitment he had made to himself and the memory of Paul. "I'm trying to pray. I'm not sure I'm very good at it, but I made a promise to my sister's husband – well, late husband – and one of my best friends, that I would try to – no, not try to – that I *would* pray every single day for a month. I guess it doesn't sound like much of a promise, but here I am. That's what brings me here, Joseph."

Joseph was silent, looking out the window as if in deep thought. Thomas waited, somewhat impatiently, for a reply. The shafts of sunlight streaming through the windows gave the small chapel the look of an ancient fairy tale. One might almost expect triumphant song to accompany the sun's glorious rays. Neither man said a word. They just sat and listened to the silence for many moments.

The old man broke the silence. "What have you heard?" Thomas didn't understand the question. What had he heard about what? Was Joseph referring to the baseball team, the college, prayer, Paul? His face must have betrayed his confusion, so his friend continued. "What songs have you heard? Where are they guiding you?"

Thomas must have still looked puzzled. Joseph's face showed no impatience or judgement. "Thomas, do you remember our first conversation? We spoke of the 'songs of a nation' and you let me know quite clearly that you didn't have time for philosophy." Of course Thomas remembered the conversation. That brief conversation had been the catalyst that set all of this into motion. Joseph's challenge had turned his life upside down, and so far, it wasn't turning out so bad. Sure, he'd get back into the business world, but for now it was a great adventure. How could he tell

Joseph all of this? He just looked at the large man, took a deep breath, and realized that Joseph already knew. How he knew this was a great puzzle for Thomas, especially when he tried to relate the chance meeting to Tiff later that night.

"Joseph, may I ask your advice on something?"

"Of course. Naturally, I cannot promise that you will like the advice or want to follow it. As a businessman, Thomas, you surely understand that." Joseph let out a deep and hearty laugh as he spoke these words and put his arm firmly on Thomas' shoulder. "Thomas, my friend, please do continue!"

"Joseph, I've been working on the 'Why?' and 'what is the real purpose?' of these new roles. It's really the same question but it comes in many forms. For example, 'What is the real goal of a baseball coach?' and 'How do you measure success as a teacher of entrepreneurship?' I think a few months ago my answers would have been simple. Win games. Help students learn how to start a business. Surely there's more to it, but that's about how I would have answered the questions. My old answers just seem to be lacking and I would love to hear your perspective."

"Now, my friend, you are looking for the right sort of thing and in the right sort of place." Joseph closed his eyes for a few long seconds before continuing. "My advice is but a simple question. 'Will you listen?'"

That was certainly not the advice Thomas expected. Over the years, Thomas had formed the habit of asking and answering his own questions before seeking advice from others. His answer to this question was more than a few words, and certainly not another question. Yet something about the old man's answer gave Thomas a sense that it contained wisdom. He just had no idea what to do with it. He sat back down, closed his eyes, and turned Joseph's words over and over in his mind. "Will you listen?" "Will I listen? - Listen for what? Listen to whom? I'm *looking for the right sort of thing in the right sort of place*." Perfect. Now all I need to do is be sure to "Listen." His eyes remained shut and his mind finally grew still and quiet. There is an answer. The words seemed crystal clear as soon as they floated across his mind. Yes, there is.

The sun must have gone behind a cloud, and Thomas could feel its warmth on his body as it reemerged. He opened his eyes and said aloud, but softly, "Yeah, there is an answer." He didn't know what it was, but was okay with that for once. Thomas looked up and then stood up abruptly, and turned to thank Joseph for the advice, advice that he may not want or follow. But the old man was not there. How long had Thomas sat there with his eyes closed? He had not even heard Joseph walk away or the chapel door open and close. So much for listening, he laughed to himself. It was time to get back to work.

The rest of the afternoon went quickly, as Thomas worked through a massive list of tasks in preparation for the baseball camp that would start in just a few weeks.

Every Day?

"Wow!" That was the only response that Tiff had for Thomas as he explained his chapel experience. Brother and sister were sitting together, watching Ryan eat an ice cream cone in the yard behind Tiff's small apartment. It was a Friday night and the school year was rapidly coming to an end. Daylight stretched well into the evening and Ryan wanted to stay up late. The two boys in Tiff's life started to kick a ball back and forth. Anyone that saw that little boy would know what kind of ice cream he had just eaten, as his face and shirt were plastered with telltale smudges of green and brown – mint chocolate chip. Tiff went inside to get a napkin. She wondered to herself, "What sort of mother lets her child look like a filthy pig?" but grabbed her phone to snap a picture of her boy in his adorable green and brown disguise.

"Uncle Tommy, can we read outside tonight?" Ryan knew that he needed to take a bath and brush his teeth before he could sit with his uncle to continue their journey through Narnia. They had already finished five of the seven books and Ryan's enthusiasm had continued to grow. The boys both looked at Tiff and she nodded her approval. Ryan ran into the house to take what must have been one of the world's fastest showers. When he came back into the yard with his pajamas practically pasted to his still-wet body and carrying a leather-bound book, his mother and uncle were in deep conversation. "I'm ready! That was so fast, right?"

He heard his uncle say, "There's something there. I've committed to giving it everything I've got for a year."

Tiff looked at her brother appreciatively. "I'll see you boys inside in a little while," she whispered as she walked into the apartment.

"What, Uncle Tommy? Give what a year?"

"Hmmmm? Oh, I was talking to your mommy about my new work. I'm going to be... helping people learn about starting a business and about baseball!"

"Awesome!! So, you're a teacher? And a coach?"

Thomas was taken back by the word teacher. "Yeah, I guess I am a teacher. But I don't really know much about teaching."

Ryan didn't even skip a beat. "I can help you. I'm a good teacher." He took his uncle's hand, guided him to sit down in the grass, hopped on his lap, and opened the book.

"Yes, you are, little man! You certainly are a good teacher!" Thomas couldn't help but nod his head and smile. How he wished he could experience being six again. But, in a way, he felt that this gift was already shared with him. Life gives you what you need, he thought. It might not give it to you in the way you would have planned it, but it certainly gives you what you need. How strange to reflect on the last few months spent with Ryan and know that it wouldn't have happened if Paul were still alive. Of course, Paul's untimely death was a tragedy. Yet this incredibly special relationship with his nephew may not have happened without that tragedy. A range of emotions that normally didn't fit together - joy and sadness, thankfulness and anger, love and grief – washed over Thomas.

"Read! C'mon Uncle Tommy!" Ryan had opened the book to where they left off and was looking up at his uncle with a sense of urgency.

"You got it buddy," Thomas said reflectively, and started to read.

Tiff was cleaning up inside, but paused by the window to look at these two boys, drifting off into an enchanted world together. She thought back to the conversation with Thomas and knew that they might only have a year before Thomas would be diving into his next company. She knew her brother. Even if he didn't go looking for it, a business venture would find him. They always had. He had connections in so many cutting-edge industries and his ability to not only see the whole picture, but to get things done, made him a very valuable partner. Someone would come calling. An investor, a partner, a former customer. Besides, the financial means of the local college were so meager compared to his standard lifestyle. She wished she could keep this new Thomas around, at least a little longer. Ryan needed it. In a moment of sheer honesty, Tiff had to admit that she needed him around, too. Sure, she was always considered strong and self-assured by family and friends, but there were many times when she didn't feel that way herself. Now was certainly one of those times. Paul was her husband. He was Ryan's father. He was "Daddy." Why had he been taken from her? How was she supposed to go forward? Tears streamed down her face as they had so many other nights. Ryan didn't see her cry. At least that's what she wanted to believe. On many nights, she had held her little six-year-old in her arms and rocked him to sleep. Holding him for hours and hours on countless nights, well after he had fallen fast asleep, had given her the comfort that she needed, had given her the will to keep trying to pull it all together. Her finances were in terrible shape. Even though Tiff and Paul were both planners, they had not planned for this. She was thankful that she had been able to sell their house quickly and move into this small and very affordable apartment.

The door opened and jolted Tiff back to the present. Ryan was excitedly chattering about everything they had just read. This brought a great smile to Tiff's face. "Me and you wouldn't run from those bullies, would we, Uncle Tommy?" The boy didn't even pause for a breath, let alone an answer. "I knew the door would open, didn't you, Uncle Tommy? It just had to open."

Thomas flashed his sister a smile and raised his eyebrows, as if to say, "This boy of yours is a bit excited!" They Thomas looked down at Ryan and asked, "How did you know – that the door would open?"

Ryan's body language practically shouted along with his reply. "It had to. It had to! Aslan! They were calling to Aslan and he *always* helps."

"Oh, he does?" Thomas asked, partly wondering about the answer himself.

"Yeah, I think." Ryan crinkled his nose and tilted his head in thought. The boy couldn't recall any time when Aslan hadn't helped.

Tiff motioned with her head towards Ryan's bedroom, so uncle and nephew made their way in that direction.

Ryan finally drifted off to sleep that evening and Thomas headed home. His night and the rest of the weekend would be very busy with preparations for the beginning of his first job running the college's summer baseball camp. He laughed in the car on the way home, thinking aloud, "How did I get here?" There was so much to do, yet so little in the way of resources. He slept very little that weekend, but interrupted his work several times for brief moments to honor his commitment to pray for ten minutes every single day. About half of his prayer time was consumed by asking himself "Will I listen?" and convincing himself that he was, indeed, listening. More than once he laughed out loud. I'm listening, but I'm just not hearing anything. That was funny to Thomas, but would not be the case for long.

Baseball Camp

Day one of summer camp went very well. Thomas was sitting at Tiff's kitchen table when she arrived home, going through notes from the day, calling to follow up with parents who had registered late, and tweaking the agenda for the next few camp days. Ryan was playing at a friend's house and would need to be picked up. Tiff headed back out to the car. Thomas was in "go-mode" and she did not want to interrupt her brother when he was on a mission. The next few days brought more of the same. Tiff planned a barbecue for Friday night, to celebrate Thomas successfully completing the first week of the camp – and surviving! She invited a few of the other coaches over as a surprise to Thomas. The assistant camp coaches were all college players who had played on the college team the season before.

Thomas and Tiff barely spoke throughout that first week of camp. Thomas was consumed with making running an excellent camp and dealing with a plethora of last-minute challenges. The college soccer team needed the field for two days that week and a campus student leadership activity wanted to be involved in the camp on another day, both of which completely disrupted Thomas' thorough plan. He dealt with it but didn't seem to be enjoying the beginning of this journey as much as Tiff had hoped.

By the time Thomas arrived at Tiff's barbecue that Friday evening, all but one of the other coaches and a few of their friends had arrived. They seemed quite pleased with the way the week had gone and were enjoying each other's company. Tiff liked hearing all the stories about the campers. It sounded like they were not only learning a lot, but having plenty of fun, as well. The mood at the barbecue was even better than Tiff had imagined, that is until Thomas walked into the backyard.

Tiff was in the kitchen getting some items for the grill. When she looked out the kitchen window, it appeared as if the party had come to an abrupt end. Everyone was quiet. Too quiet. She walked back into the yard and saw Thomas standing next to one of the player-coaches, a kid who must have been about twenty years old named Willie. The group that had been standing nearby quickly and quietly drifted away from this corner of the yard. The young man had been one of the liveliest story tellers just a few moments before, but now remained eerily silent, his head bent, as if ashamed. Tiff didn't hear any of the words her brother and this athlete exchanged, but it wasn't long before her brother repeated the interaction with another of his young assistants.

"Thomas." She called to her brother from the grill. "Thomas! I really need your help for a second on the grill." She knew *that he knew* that she didn't really need help grilling, so she tried to think of the best way to keep him there long enough to have a conversation. When her brother made his way over to the grill, she locked eyes with him and said with a soft but intense voice, "Will you listen?" That got Thomas' attention. She knew that she needed to shift his focus so that they could have this conversation without deflating the party's energy any further. "Some very good things happened this week." She nodded her head with warm approval. "Thomas, I want to thank you. More than that, I want you to know that I'm proud of you."

"Yeah. The week was okay." Thomas wasn't one to accept praise very readily. Besides, he didn't think the week went all that well. As usual, his standards were significantly different from the majority of the world around him.

"Thomas. I want to tell you this. I think you need to hear it. Can you listen to me for just a minute?" She had raised her intensity. Tiff wasn't always comfortable speaking this boldly, but she knew that this message was important. She paused for a long moment, trying to decide on the best way to approach this. Finally, she decided that it might be best to buy some time. "Thomas, let's talk more after the barbecue. For now, can I make a request, as your sister? Can you: one – genuinely try to have a good time tonight and two – only talk about the things that went well at camp this week? Just for tonight? Can you do that for me?"

Thomas could tell that his sister was serious about these requests. "Okay," he muttered. "But we'll talk later. You know how much..." Tiff cut him off mid-sentence by pointing at Ryan. One of the young assistants that Thomas had just spoken with was chasing Ryan around the yard with a dodgeball. The two were competing so fiercely that they almost knocked over the beverage table. Before he had the chance to violate his promise, Tiff held up one finger and mouthed the word "One" and "Have fun!" She then held up a second finger and mouthed "Two... Good stuff." Her face alternated from that sisterly teasing smile to her "you'd better listen or there will be trouble" look. At that moment, the ball landed near Thomas' feet. He bent over and picked up the ball just in time to see Willie's face transform from joy to solemnity. The next instant, Ryan had knocked the ball away from Thomas and was sprinting away at full speed. This little guy's contagious burst of laughter infected both Thomas and young Coach Willie. As Ryan speedily turned around the corner of the house and disappeared from view, both Thomas and Willie sprinted after him. Several laps and sharp turns later, they all paused to catch their breath and shared a good laugh together. Thomas and Willie talked about a strategy to catch Ryan for a few brief minutes while Ryan hid on the other side of the house. It felt different and was a connection they both needed. Thomas finally picked up the ball to continue the game.

Will You Listen?

Tiff looked content, sitting on a bench in the backyard and reflecting on the week. Thomas sat down next to her, asking, "Do you mind if I join you?" He had just returned from reading to Ryan, but that didn't last long after Ryan's very busy and active week. Thomas had not wanted to put the book down, but Ryan was fast asleep within a few minutes.

"Ya done good, kid!" Thomas looked at his sister and continued, "Thank you for everything."

She nodded in silent acknowledgement.

After a long silence, a silence that is only comfortable between two who know each other as well as these siblings, Thomas asked, "What's going on in that mind of yours, Tiff?"

"A lot of thoughts," she said reflectively. "But first, tell me about Narnia. What is the latest adventure? Ryan is always filling me in, but the stories aren't always in order!"

Thomas loved to re-count the stories to his sister. Over the last few months, it had become a part of their weekly routine. At least once a week, Thomas would fill her in on the adventures. He really enjoyed this. It helped him become even more involved in the story, got him to reflect on what was happening, and he welcomed his sister's insightful observations and questions.

As Thomas filled Tiff in on the beginning of Book 6, *The Silver Chair*, she listened with the same amazing interest she always showed. Somehow, he thought, my sister is always able to truly pay attention, even if she's got a thousand distracting thoughts and projects. She zones everything out and listens attentively. Although he had experienced her attentive listening many times before, on this evening he paused to reflect on it. It must be a choice. Tiff must actively choose to listen, to zone out distractions. A simple choice. It surprised him to realize that he had never thought about this before. He was even more appreciative of his

66

sister when he considered the price of choosing to ignore distractions in order to focus on the person in front of her. Thomas paused his recap and stared into the night sky as he asked himself how few times he had given someone the same gift of full rapt attention. Joseph's challenge of "Will you Listen?" reverberated in his mind. Powerful, yet full of deep wisdom and concern. Was this what his friend had meant?

Tiff's voice interrupted the quiet and brought Thomas back from his search for instances when he had truly listened to others. "I want to know the words… Thomas, would you get the book and read his words to me?"

"Thomas," she repeated softly, "Can you bring your book out here?"

"Yes." He walked quietly into Ryan's room to get the book from the little guy's night stand.

As he sat back down next to Tiff, he flipped through the pages looking for the things that stood out.

"Here – 'You would not have called to me unless I had been calling to you.' The lion said that to Jill, but she was confused. She had not heard anyone calling to her. Hold on, let me find it…." He flipped back a few pages, excitedly searching for something that he wanted to share with Tiff. "Yes! Listen to this – they are trying to get to Narnia and have this idea to stand a certain way and recite a charm or spell. But then the boy who had been there before – remember Eustace from the last book, about the boat, the *Dawn Treader*? He, Eustace, confides in his new friend Jill about Aslan. They are about to make magic signs and incantations when Eustace says, 'I don't think he'd like them. It would look as if we thought we could make him do things. But really, we can only ask him.' Tiff, remember, in the other books, when they said Aslan was not a tame lion? They said he was good, but not tame. He's unpredictable. There's something wild about him. He doesn't simply do what you want or really what you might wish he would do. But it works out. I think that's one of the crazy things in these books. You know that Aslan could just make things work if he wanted to, but he rarely shows up when you want or does things the way you want."

Tiff was listening, but was also laughing out loud now. "Are you listening, my wonderful brother? Are you listening to what you've just said?"

"Of course, I'm listening. What do you mean?" Thomas was rarely happy to be straightened out by anyone, including his sister.

"Aslan guides them, but they don't always listen or choose to hear and follow his guidance. He helps them, but rarely in ways that follow their plans or schedules. He calls them, but they seem to think that they were doing the calling."

Thomas nodded in agreement but didn't seem ready to weigh the consequences of this thought process to his own life just yet.

She continued, "May I ask, for what did Aslan call them to Narnia this time?" She took the book from Thomas' lap and began flipping through the first twenty or thirty pages, searching out the conversation between the Lion and the girl.

Thomas was happy that her question brought their discussion back to Narnia, to the book, and away from his unwillingness to listen. "We were just getting there when I noticed that Ryan had fallen asleep. Their mission is to rescue a prince. Aslan will give them four signs to guide their journey. The lion didn't explain much more about the mission, but made Jill repeat the four signs to him. She thought she had them, but didn't. He made sure she was clear about these simple, although rather vague, instructions. That's where I stopped reading tonight... but I'll re-read some of that tomorrow with Ryan." Thomas pointed to the bottom of the page of the book Tiff held open between them. She looked at Aslan's words and re-read sections of the dialogue leading up to this point.

"Look at this! Thomas, right there." She pointed to the middle of a page and read Aslan's words aloud, "'That is a very good answer, Human Child. Do so no more.... Your task will be the harder because of what you have done.' See that? He knows exactly what she has done, but he asks her about it. When she admits her poor choice to him, he doesn't just go easy on her. He tells her to 'do so no more' and gives her a harder task because of her poor choice. Oh, he's good!" She had that motherly smile now, the one she frequently wore after an interaction with Ryan that she felt went extremely well.

"Good stuff," was Thomas' reply to Tiff's excitement.

Her speech quickened. "Thomas, do you see it? That's it. That's what I was talking about earlier. Are you hearing me now? That's what I meant when I asked you if you will listen! Thomas, I've been thinking about this all week. Remember all the quotes you sent me from the Narnia author, C. S. Lewis. I've been looking through them. He was a wise man. Someone to listen to. His words – and his stories – are full of wisdom, for anyone who will listen." She looked up at Thomas as she said these last words and he let them sink in. Her look wasn't one of accusation or condemnation. Rather, it was a look of one who was on the same journey, and just wanted to share an insight with a fellow traveler. Someone who wanted to help him make the trip but also knew that she, herself, also needed plenty of help. Rather than a harsh judgement, it felt more like the caring words of one who recommends packing an extra bottle of water for a hike to account for the humidity.

Tiff continued, "Your encounters with Joseph... he's asked you some very significant questions. There are three that stand out most to me are: "Whose words do you let affect your life?" "What are you looking for?" and "Will you listen?" When we really dig into these children's books, his wisdom is woven throughout. It doesn't always jump out at you unless you look for it and slow down to listen. Do you see, Thomas? If you let all three of Joseph's questions guide you, the answers start to appear."

"Hmm." Thomas often used this expression to create a pause, to create space. Tiff could see that he was evaluating whether he wanted to go deeper into this conversation or not. "So, you liked the quotes?" Thomas asked. "Do you have a favorite? I have to admit, I've come across so many as I read his works and searched online. But I haven't taken much time to go through them. Which did you like?"

"Thomas, there are so many. One that grabbed me and comes to mind right now: 'Human history is the long terrible story of man trying to find something other than God which will make him happy.'"

She didn't need to repeat these words. Thomas had reread them a dozen times when he first came across the expression weeks ago. He just sat there and stared up into the starlit sky as Tiff excused herself to get something from inside the house.

When she returned, Tiff brought several pages of handwritten notes. "Before we talk about the quotes, Thomas, I think I owe you the continuation of an earlier conversation." When she slowed down and her words were calculated, Thomas knew that the topic was both uncomfortable and important. "Thomas, I noticed that you had a few conversations with your assistants at the barbecue this evening. Did they have the effect you wanted?"

While Thomas knew this conversation was coming at some point, he had hoped they could stay on Narnia for a while longer. In one of his classic attempts to dismiss the topic or delay it until some future date, Thomas offhandedly quipped, "Who knows. I guess we'll find out over the next week or so."

Tiff looked at her brother, even though he avoided her eye contact. She was searching for the best way to get through to him without pushing any buttons that might have him driving away. She looked down at her notes in one hand and the book in the other. A few long moments passed. Tiff opened the book and looked through the Lion's words again. "That's it!" She had not meant to say this aloud, but was surprised to see how obvious the answer was. "Thomas, what are you looking for with the assistant coaches, with – what was the young man's name, wasn't it Will or Willie? Yes, Willie! What are you looking for, or what do you expect from Willie?"

"I guess…" Thomas began slowly, "I guess I want Willie – well all of them – to take responsibility for creating a great experience at the camp. Well, that's not all. I want them to step back and evaluate the activities, the set-ups, the drills, the coaching moments. Yeah, they should know what we're trying to do and get it done… and make it better. Pretty basic."

"Thomas," Tiff was quietly laughing by this point, but Thomas looked very serious and had not yet noticed her laughter. "Yeah, basic. Simple. They should just do everything the way you do it, right?"

Even though her quiet laughter could be heard through her voice, Thomas didn't seem to notice. He replied, "Yup. Not so complicated at all. Why doesn't it happen?" As he said this, he stared out into the darkness of the backyard. Then he turned his head toward Tiff and her laughing smile woke him up to the humor of what he had just described. Suddenly, the two were absolutely cracking up with a contagious and joyous laughter most often brought about with the humility of laughing at one's self.

Tiff finally spoke again, "Can we try an experiment? Let's use Joseph's three questions. First, whose words do you let affect your life? Let's start with letting Joseph and C.S. Lewis' words affect us. The answer to the second question, 'What are we looking for?' might be a lesson, principle, guidance, even a truth. Let's try that. How did your friend Joseph get you thinking without creating too much resistance? Is there a principle there?"

Thomas realized that he had really missed the perspective that his sister provided. He appreciated their recent reconnection, despite the deeply saddening circumstances that brought it about.

He wondered for a moment why he had let so much time pass without nurturing his relationship with his incredible sister.

"Well?" She interrupted his reflection.

"Perhaps you should go first, my wise sister!" he leaned forward and tilted his head, which rested in his hands while his elbows propped up his arms from their resting place on his knees. It was the perfect position to say, "Your student is ready for his lesson, oh wise one."

"Joseph asks questions. They are not condescending, leading, or manipulative, but they do cut through and clarify. They capture your attention. Not only capture, they keep your attention. And they let you know that the asker has some wisdom, that the asker understands something about your situation or even about the way the world works. Thomas, look at what Aslan says here." She held the book open, pointing to a few sentences. "Your Lion essentially asked the girl, Jill, three consecutive questions: 'Where is the boy?' 'How did he fall?' and 'Why were you there?' Simple questions with no accusatory tone. But, they made it clear that she had done wrong, that there was an error in judgment on Jill's part, and that Aslan knew about it. The questions also lead to Aslan telling the girl, 'Do so no more' – stop showing off!"

Thomas looked at Tiff with great admiration. This was a fairy tale, but she had just extracted wisdom from its pages. What impressed him most is that she hadn't even read the book, just flipped through a few pages to find this powerful lesson. He almost shouted, "What are you looking for? Will you listen? That's it. I was reading and certainly paying attention, but I couldn't honestly say I've been looking for anything more than an entertaining story. And, as a result, I certainly wasn't listening for the lessons it had for me."

"Thomas, I have to get to bed. It was a long week and I know Ryan will be up early, ready to show me some of those baseball skills he's been learning at your camp." She reached out and handed him the papers with her favorite C.S. Lewis quotes. "These are a few of my favorites. Let me know if any of them speak to you the next time we talk!"

While Thomas nodded in agreement, he had no idea at the time just how much those papers would speak to him over the coming days.

A Surprise Encounter

Thomas was awake before the sun that Saturday morning. He wanted to review the first week's camp experience and modify the game plan in anticipation of week two. After a light breakfast, he brought his laptop, pile of notes, and coffee down to the park. Within a few minutes, he was sitting at a picnic table by the river, totally engrossed in analyzing the week's lessons on how to run a baseball camp. Although he had plenty of experience hiring and managing people, these young kids that comprised his camp staff were different. He thought it might be their age, or the simple fact that they didn't really work for him, of maybe that it was just a short-term summer job. Was this just a forgone conclusion, a reality of running a summer camp? How would – or could – he get them to be a little more motivated, to take more responsibility? Thomas was in business mode and didn't even notice the woman standing next to him.

"Looks like a serious project," she said, as she tapped him lightly on the shoulder. Thomas was almost in a trance; such was his focus on the project of summer baseball camp. As he looked up, the woman was surprised at the intensity in his eyes. But when he saw who it was, his face softened and he leaned back from the laptop.

"What a nice surprise! What brings you here?" Thomas rarely liked to be interrupted when he was getting things done, but he was genuinely happy to see Clara standing next to him.

"It's summer! School's out and my son loves this park. What about you? It looks like you've set up an office here. I certainly don't want to interrupt."

Thomas relaxed his body a bit more, hoping Clara wouldn't think he was trying to end a conversation that hadn't even begun. He motioned at the papers and laptop spread across the table, shrugged his shoulders, and joked, "Oh this? It's just my idea of a fun Saturday morning."

Clara laughed. "I suppose everyone needs a hobby!" They shared a brief smile, which she translated into permission to continue teasing him. "And how shall we describe this hobby of yours? Turning picnic tables by the river on a peaceful Saturday morning into the corner office? Maybe it needs a formal name?" Clara's face clearly indicated that she wanted him to join in her jest.

"How about," Thomas paused for effect, "Office on the Green?"

She smiled at his suggestion. "It's been a while since we've bumped into each other." Clara was thinking of their first conversation and the few rushed interactions they'd had at drop-off or pick-up in the elementary school parking lot since. Life can be so busy, she thought. She wondered if Thomas remembered her thirty seconds on the philosophy of life. Instead of asking, she kept it light. "What's got your attention these days? Or, as Thoreau put it, 'What are you busy about?'"

"Good question! Actually, one thing that's got my attention lately is just that – the questions that we chase, maybe your friend Thoreau would say 'the questions we are busy about!' So many things have been keeping my attention. I have a new job – well, to be more accurate, it's more like three new jobs." Thomas was amazed at how comfortable he felt sharing this with her. He typically kept so much of his plans, experiences, and thoughts to himself. Clara smiled as he spoke, encouraging him to continue. "It's crazy! I've never really had a job before… well, I mean I've been in my own businesses, so I've never been employed."

He didn't want her to think that he didn't work and was about to explain this a bit more in depth, but she interjected, "Yup. I know what you mean," and then nodded for him to carry on.

"Out of the blue, I ended up working for the college. I'm teaching, coaching, and helping them build an entrepreneurship program – oh," he almost forgot to add the current pressing situation, "and running the summer baseball camp."

"Amazing!" Clara seemed genuinely excited as she said it. "Summer baseball camp – is that for the college players?"

Thomas didn't skip a beat. "Oh no. The program is designed for children of all ages and skill levels. Our camp staff are excellent at assessing the…" Before she interrupted, Thomas was practically reciting the camp brochures, and for good reason. He had designed or overhauled all of them.

"You're good! Are you telling me that you just started these new jobs? It sounds like you've been doing this camp for years!" She was kidding, but also quite impressed to see just how *in to* this new position Thomas already was.

"Yeah, right!" Thomas shot back. "It definitely feels like I've been doing it for a few years already. Honestly, though, I feel okay about it, but at times it really feels like I might be in over my head."

"Come on, Thomas! You've only just begun. Of course it will feel a little overwhelming in the beginning. From the sound of it – and the look of this picnic table office – you'll be a master of this summer camp operation in another few days!" She sounded business-like, yet was smiling at the same time. This quality was one Thomas wished he could execute a lot better.

"We'll see," was all he could reply.

"Thomas, are all the jobs with the college?"

"Yes. It's really just one job with a few separate functions. Do I make it sound like a big complicated ordeal?"

"Oh no. Not at all," Clara replied. She said it with a teasing tone and expression that had him laughing. "I have an uncle that used to work for the college. He's officially retired, but still involved somehow." Clara's face lit up and she exclaimed, "The camp! Do you have any openings for a younger boy? He's six and doesn't really have much baseball experience. But he really does like baseball!" Thomas' body language and the expression on his face betrayed him. Clara picked up on his response instantly, saying, "If it's too late, I completely understand. I wish I had known earlier. I don't want..."

Thomas cut in. "No, it's fine. We can handle another camper." He tried to shake the initial negative response out of his mind, but the policies for the camp were one of the big issues he had been working through that morning at his picnic table office. He had modified the document for his team to make sure everyone was clear about coach to player ratios for age groups, policies for joining the camp late, and all sorts of other scenarios. He wanted this camp to be perfect and had written up just about every scenario he could imagine for his assistant coaches. Adding another child in the youngest age group after week 1 would go against the policies he had written up. Thomas knew that his facial expression and tone of voice clearly communicated one word: *inconvenience.*

"Thomas, it's really okay. Maybe next time around." Clara unsuccessfully tried to hide her disappointment. She had let herself get excited about the idea of her little guy playing baseball. She knew he would love it, but certainly did not want to impose on Thomas. "We've got so many things going on this summer. It probably wouldn't fit the schedule anyway."

By this point, Thomas was rationalizing a change in the rules. He raised his eyebrows and held up the index finger of each hand to get Clara's attention. "Consider him signed up. Come to think of it, we get a few sponsors that provide full scholarships to the camp each summer and I realized that we still have one available. Monday morning. If you can get there a little before camp starts, I'll give him a crash course on what we've been doing so he won't feel left out when the other kids arrive."

Clara was so excited that she gave Thomas a big hug and said, "Thank you! Thank you so much! I can get him there early on Monday. He will be so, so excited!" Her eyes were full of gratitude.

The Rules

Thomas was sitting at the picnic table all alone. Clara had things to take care of and had departed, but not before giving Thomas a second hug. He was just sitting and staring off across the river for what must have been several minutes when a light breeze blew several papers off the table. Thomas jumped up and ran to retrieve the papers. As he walked back to his park *office*, he looked down at the papers he had just retrieved. One of them was covered with Tiff's handwriting. It was one of her papers full of quotes from C. S. Lewis. He read through a few dozen quotes, but three captured his attention that morning:

- "I can't imagine a man really enjoying a book and reading it only once."
- "Education without values, as useful as it is, seems rather to make man a more clever devil."
- "If you look for truth, you may find comfort in the end; if you look for comfort you will not get either comfort or truth only soft soap and wishful thinking to begin, and in the end, despair."

As he sat back down and secured the papers against another gust of wind, Thomas typed the three quotes into the introduction of his "Summer Baseball Camp Policies" guide book. Without thinking about it, he decided to also type in the three questions that he and Tiff had discussed the night before. They didn't seem to belong in the policy book, but he had the file open and wanted to capture these thoughts.

Back to work, he thought to himself. Thomas looked through his notes on the drills and timing of each activity. They all needed some serious attention. The next few hours were spent enhancing this aspect of the camp. Saturday morning and the rest of the weekend would fly by. By Sunday night, Thomas thought he was ready for Monday morning and the beginning of Week 2.

Week 2, Ready or Not?

He was not the first to arrive at the field. He thought he would be, and was quite surprised to see the equipment already set up at the stations. That took some serious effort, thought Thomas. He wondered who could have done it? He didn't wonder for long, and was surprised to see Willie and two of the other assistant coaches come out of the dugout, each carrying a large water jug. Thomas looked across the field, mentally noting that everything was ready to go. He had expected to be busy for the next hour doing exactly what his assistants had already done.

The boys acknowledged Thomas with a "Hey coach! We're ready for the campers." Thomas walked over to Willie, and was about to apologize for being so harsh on the young man that past Friday at Tiff's barbecue. Before he had the chance to say anything, Willie said, "Coach, do you have a second?" and motioned for Thomas to walk with him towards the batting cage. As they walked, Thomas was thinking through what he should say to the young man. But Willie spoke first. "Coach, I owe you an apology." Thomas wasn't expecting this, and the young ballplayer continued. "You were right. I needed to be called out. I didn't give it my all last week. I was thinking about it over the weekend and realized that you had too much of the workload."

Thomas started to respond, "Willie..." but the young man held up his hand, as if asking permission to speak.

"Coach, I talked with the other guys and we're going to step up. You were dead on, we need to be more responsible, to take more initiative, to take a good hard look at how the camp is going and make some changes."

By this time, Thomas was shocked. After his conversation with Tiff on Friday night, a big part of his focus over the rest of the weekend was on how to get these guys on board, how to more clearly communicate expectations and gain their commitment to meeting those expectations. He knew he wasn't exactly polite in his conversation with Willie on Friday, but now, just a few days later and without any patching up of the relationship, Willie was taking the initiative. Thomas thought that perhaps Tiff had been wrong in accusing him of being too blunt. No, Tiff, that's what people really need, Thomas thought. It had worked, after all.

Thomas thought about his policy book and wondered if much of it might not be necessary. He had printed copies for each of the assistants and they were sitting in a box on the floor of his convertible. Would he distribute them? Yes. So much of the basic flow of the drills was mapped out. He walked back to his car to get the books and handed them to each assistant. They had enough time to read through the books before the campers started to arrive.

The assistant coaches read through their new handbooks on the bleachers by the field. Thomas walked to the outfield, rethinking his weekend's work. Before he got very far, he heard a car door close. When he looked towards the parking lot, he saw Clara walking towards him with her six-year-old son. Thomas walked briskly towards them.

"Joey, this is Coach Thomas. You've met before. Remember? He's Ryan's uncle." She turned towards Thomas. "Ryan will be here later, right?"

"Yes, Ryan will should be getting here soon. Joey? Good to have you here at camp. You like baseball?"

The little guy stayed close to his mother, but nodded and made an "Uh huh" sound without looking Thomas in the eyes.

"Joey, mommy has to go to work now. The coach is going to show you some of the fun things the kids do to practice baseball." She turned to Thomas and said, "Thank you again. Thank you so much!" Then Clara turned and walked briskly back to her car, leaving Joey standing there with his hands in his pockets, looking at the ground. As Clara got into her beat up little car and drove away, Thomas took in a deep breath and slowly exhaled, thinking about the long first few days of week one, especially trying to be patient with the youngest kids who cried for their mommies and daddies sporadically throughout the days. It reminded him of dominoes, the way one child would ask about a parent, then another, and another. Dominoes. Now that most of the young campers were getting pretty good at making it through the days, he and the coaching staff had another newbie. Thomas pushed his anticipatory thoughts about another round of domino crying to the back of his mind as he stepped closer to Joey. He crouched down and held out a ball to this little person. Joey didn't look up, but he did reach out to take the ball. Good first step.

"Think you could hit that garbage can with the ball?" Thomas asked. "Give it a toss."

Joey shifted his glance upward just slightly, just enough to see the garbage can about fifteen feet away. Thomas could see a few tear streaks on the boy's cheeks, but a tiny smile crept onto the little face. It was only a partial smile, hindered by the boy clenching his teeth in determination. His eyes zoned in on the garbage can and his nose crinkled like a tiger that knew its prey was all but finished. Without warning, Joey unleashed the ball and it sailed over the garbage can. Not a bad throw, thought Coach Thomas.

"Want another try," Thomas held out another baseball to the boy, who readily took it from his hand while only taking his eye off the target long enough to look towards the coach, grab the ball, and nod. The second throw was pretty good, too.

"Who taught you to throw like that?" Thomas asked, trying to sound like he was very impressed.

The boy didn't say anything, but just shrugged his shoulders and reached for the third baseball that Thomas was holding out for him. Joey's next few throws were right on line, hitting the plastic garbage can with a Thud!

"Yes!" shouted little Joey, along with an abbreviated fist pump. Thomas held his hand up for a high five, and the boy slapped his new coach's hand with some force.

Thomas led his new ball player around to several other stations on the field before the other campers began to arrive. This kid had some good natural ability and it seemed that someone must have taught him some basic skills. The initial concerns that Thomas had that morning about taking on a late addition to the camp started to fade.

All in all, the first day of week two went well. Except, that is, for the attitude one assistant had about the new handbook. This particular assistant was not among those who showed up extra early that morning to take care of the set-up. At the stations where he was assigned, he kept running drills the way they had during the first week. His stations were among those that Thomas had completely redesigned over the weekend and the new way was mapped out in full detail in the handbook.

The first time Thomas noticed was just before lunch. He had approached the young assistant, Ben, who would be entering his sophomore year at the college that fall. When Ben looked up, the coach was already standing next to him with a handbook opened to the page that outlined his station's activities.

"We changed it up a bit. Not sure if you had the chance to read this yet," Thomas said as he handed the open book to Ben. Thomas turned rather abruptly and walked away.

About twenty minutes later, before blowing the whistle and announcing lunch, Thomas looked towards Ben's stations once again. Nothing had changed. He was still doing everything the old way. Thomas was not happy and vowed to straighten this out during lunch.

"Ben... Please take a few minutes to re-read that section and then come talk to me." Thomas said it coldly, abruptly, and then walked away from Ben's lunch spot under a tall maple tree.

While eating his own lunch, Thomas read through the same segment of the handbook, occasionally nodding in agreement with the process he had put together over the weekend. The process laid out in the book was much better than the way Ben was running this drill. Players would get two or three times as many swings and there was an enhanced focus built into the revised drill procedure. Surely Ben just needed to read it and then he would agree. And if he didn't, Thomas would give him a warning. That was how it would go.

"You said you wanted to see me, Coach?" Thomas looked up from his sandwich and realized that his face probably still had the smug expression of one who knows he's right.

"Yeah. Have a seat."

Ben sat in the grass next to his boss and future college baseball coach, if it would last that long. Ben had heard that this new guy was once a local baseball star who was just taking a break from his business career. Through the years, Ben had met many coaches and had worn so many of them out. Although he was a phenomenally talented ballplayer, everywhere he had played, rumors always swirled that he was un-coachable. Sure, Ben had heard the rumors, but didn't really agree with them. He just had some bad coaches. If the coach knew what he was doing, Ben told himself, he would be more than happy to listen.

Thomas asked, "Did you get through the section on your drills?"

"Yeah."

"Any questions?"

"No. It's pretty straightforward."

On one hand, Thomas was hoping for a dialogue, but Ben seemed uninterested. On the other hand, Thomas was happy to get back to finishing his lunch and making some other adjustments for the afternoon.

Ben got to his feet and stood there for a moment before asking, "Are we good? Was there anything else?"

"We're good." Thomas felt an edge, an iciness from this young man before he turned and walked away.

Thomas stood up and walked towards the youngest group. He wanted to see how Joey was doing. The boy was sitting all by himself, glumly staring at his food. Before Thomas reached him, he saw a baseball rolling towards Joey's feet. Thomas stopped walking and followed the path of the ball backwards, only to see Willie hiding his head in his hands. Willie's goofy laugh billowed out from his partly hidden face. Joey picked up the ball and looked around, searching to find who had rolled or dropped it. Suddenly he spotted Willie and his once glum face immediately brightened.

"You! Coach Willie, I know it was you!"

Coach Willie poked his head out from behind his hands, making a face that said, *"I don't know what you're talking about."*

"Me?" Willie asked, shrugging his shoulders and pointing both index fingers at himself in disbelief.

Joey stared at him and slowly raised his right arm to point at his new friend. "Yeah, you." He started walking towards the assistant coach, first slowly and deliberately, but picking up the pace with every few steps. Willie was shaking his head and mouthing the word *No*, but Joey just countered by nodding his head and mouthing *Yes*. Within seconds, Willie had leapt up and was walking quickly, almost jogging, away from Joey. Suddenly, the chase was on. Thomas was still standing there watching as the two darted around the field and drill stations. The small boy would get close to catching his assistant coach, but Willie would make a narrow escape. Finally, Joey had Coach Willie cornered near the backstop. Thomas heard Willie say, "You'll never take me alive!" as he made a mad dash and feigned an attempt to run through the six-year-old. Joey had a frightened look for just a moment, but closed his eyes and lunged at the much bigger Coach Willie. When Joey opened his eyes, he realized that he had wrapped his arms around Willie's legs and tackled him to the ground. Victory!

"I told you, Coach Willie! You are my prisoner, now." Joey beamed as Willie said, "I give up. I give up!"

Lunchtime ended, and it was time to get the afternoon sessions going. As the campers and assistant coaches got started at their stations, Thomas tried to inconspicuously sneak a glance at Ben's station. It looked like Ben was using the new process. Good. Thomas had enough to focus on without a staff insubordination problem.

The afternoon sessions went extremely well, and Thomas was almost content with the improvements. Rare was the day when Thomas was perfectly content, so almost content was a pretty good place to be.

As the parents came to pick up their kids, Thomas realized that he kept perking up every time another car pulled in, checking to see if it was Clara's. He was busy getting the equipment put away when he looked up and saw Joey waving goodbye from the back of a different car. Joey was waving to Coach Willie.

Thomas took a break from his clean up and called over to Coach Willie, "Is Joey getting a ride with someone else? That wasn't his mother's car. I mean, is Joey getting a ride with another parent..."

Willie raised his eyebrows and tilted his face into a look of curiosity. "His grandfather. Coach, Joey's grandfather picked him up. No worries, coach. He's on the approved pick-up list. Anyway, the little fella did great today, especially for his first day! Why all the concern? You counting on the kid becoming one of your future college star players?"

Thomas laughed and said, "Thanks, I was just checking. It's nothing – I just know his mother and told her we'd take good care of him."

Willie winked and said, "Yup, that's what I was thinking."

Thomas just shook his head and went back to getting the equipment together.

It's not About Fair

When they arrived at Tiff's house, Thomas realized that he hadn't even spoken to his sister since Friday night. She had sent him several text messages, but he was so consumed in getting things together that he had ignored just about everything else. They parked in Tiff's driveway and Ryan spoke up from the back seat, "Do you have time to read tonight, Uncle Tommy?"

They had not spoken on the ride from the baseball field and Thomas realized that he had barely talked to Ryan all day. Not only that, but he didn't see him at all over the weekend, except for Friday night.

"Sure, buddy. Sure. We'll read tonight." Thomas felt a twinge of remorse for being busy the last few days.

Thomas stuck around for dinner. Ryan only occasionally stopped talking long enough to catch his breath as he filled his mother in on the events of baseball camp. He was having so much fun. Thomas was only partially listening. The camp felt more like one of his business ventures now. He was working out the bugs, figuring out the processes, analyzing the "customer interaction" points, optimizing. It will be a very good camp, he thought to himself. It's not there yet, but I'll get it there.

Thomas' thoughts were interrupted by Ryan tugging at his arm. "Ryan, we don't tug on arms at the dinner table. Please say excuse me to Uncle Tommy." If there were ever a textbook written on parenting that Thomas might consider reading, Tiff would have to be the author!

"Uncle Tommy, excuse me, please." Ryan was trying to be patient and polite, but he had something that he just needed to say to his uncle.

"Uncle Tommy, didn't I crush the ball in the four-on-four game? Didn't I?"

"Oh yeah, buddy! You really crushed it." Ryan was beaming as Thomas affirmed his baseball heroics. He looked at Tiff and continued, "Ryan hit it even further than some of the seven- and eight- year-olds. This guy can hit!"

"See, Mom? I told you. You should come to camp. Can you? Can you take off from work to see me at camp?"

Tiff had to smile at this. She was so happy to see her son in high spirits. "I'll talk to my boss and see if I can take a long lunch break one day, okay buddy? I'm so proud of you."

After dinner and Ryan's bath, Thomas kept his promise and they read two chapters. When Ryan fell asleep, Thomas carried the book with him into the kitchen, only to find Tiff sobbing at the table. Her head was in her hands and Thomas could tell that she had been sitting that way for quite some time. He had planned to get home early to catch up on some sleep, but Tiff needed him.

"Hey, you okay, kid?" Thomas knew this might not be the best choice of words, but he just never seemed to know how to deal with others' grief.

She didn't look up, only mumbled, "I'm okay."

He let a few moments pass and then asked, "You sure?"

"Yes," Tiff said quietly, followed by, "No. I mean No. I'm not really okay."

Although he knew she wasn't okay, Thomas had secretly hoped that she would have stuck with the Yes, the answer that he, himself, would give if their circumstances were flipped. He always said he was okay, regardless of the reality. Why pull someone else into your problems – at least that was the way he rationalized it.

"Tiff, what are you thinking about?"

She didn't respond.

"We don't have to talk about it if you don't want to." Thomas offered.

"Thomas, I... I can't... I just miss him. Sometimes it just doesn't seem fair. Why does my Ryan have to grow up without a dad?" She was sobbing again. Thomas had no idea if he should try to offer some advice, just say nothing, agree, or something else.

He finally opened his mouth, "Tiff, I know. I know." He hugged his sister tightly. Thomas didn't let many emotions get the best of him, but right now, he felt washed in both anger and a sense that his sister was right. This was not fair. Ryan needed a dad. This shouldn't have happened, not to his sister, not to his friend, not to his nephew. He loved that little guy so much. Minutes passed without either speaking. Then Tiff straightened up, wiped the tears from her cheeks and eyes, and closed her eyes as if collecting herself.

"Do you still have my quotes?" Thomas was surprised that she asked this. "I don't need them back; I have my own copy. I was just wondering if you had the chance to look at them at all."

"Tiff – well, I've been…" he was thinking about how many times since Saturday he had revisited his sister's list.

"I know; you've been pretty busy. It's just that…" before Tiff could finish her sentence, Thomas had taken folded up papers out of his pocket and put them on the table. She looked down at her own handwriting and Thomas' notes in the margins. "Oh," she said in surprise. In her shock at Thomas having the quotes with him, she had forgotten what she was about to say.

"It's just that…?" Thomas looked at her and waited for her to remember her train of thought.

"Oh, yes. Thank you, Thomas." Tiff looked at the wall and continued, "It's just that he – C.S. Lewis – wrote some things that, well… let me put it this way. I remember a philosophy professor from college who often said, *'The truth always sounds sweet to the ears.'* Does that make any sense to you?"

"Yes," Thomas responded, and was deep in thought. He had to remind himself to listen to his sister, even though what she had just said sparked a thought that he would need to ponder later. "Yes, it does."

"Well," Tiff put her hand on her forehead and leaned forward. She looked up at Thomas to make sure they connected on this point. "I guess it's just that Lewis writes some things that I just know are true and I know that I need to hear them. I don't necessarily like them. But that doesn't matter. They're right. They're true. They sound sweet to the ear, but part of me wants to be mad. Part of me wants them not to be true, or just not to apply to me and my life right now." She paused again, and Thomas could tell that she had been thinking about this for some time. "Thomas, can I show you a quote that has really rattled my perspective over the last few days?"

Thomas nodded. He wasn't sure if she wanted him to say something as she was looking through the papers he had placed on the table. When she pointed at the line, he knew it immediately. He had written several bold question marks in front of the quote.

"Here. This is it: *'God allows us to experience the low points of life in order to teach us lessons that we could learn in no other way.'*"

Thomas had read and re-read this phrase more than a dozen times over the last few days. He was torn. In so many ways he completely understood the message, but, at the same time, he wasn't sure that he wanted it to be altogether true.

Tiff paused to let the words sink in, then continued, "Wisdom distilled." She closed her eyes.

The two sat together silently for a while as they finished their tea – Thomas with his big mug and Tiff with her dainty cup – Tiff assured her brother that she would be okay, and they said their goodnights.

Good isn't Good Enough

By that Friday, Thomas was more than ready for the weekend. Much of the week had been excellent, but he wasn't satisfied. The camp had certainly become like most of his projects. It consumed him. It simply had to be excellent, had to be the best summer baseball camp around. That was a given.

While Willie and several of the assistant coaches had continued to help considerably with the set-up, the staff's collective energy level had dipped noticeably. Thomas also had some concern about the coaches' attitudes. But there was a bigger issue this week. Ben. Talk about having a chip on your shoulder, this kid really carried an attitude around with him. And it rubbed off a little too much. Thomas was ready to do something about it. But what?

Thomas tried not to talk about it during dinner that evening. He, Tiff, and Ryan were at the local pizzeria. Ryan was still bubbling over, describing all the spectacular plays, mishaps, and funny moments of the week. They shared a large plain pizza. Thomas looked at simple meal and reminisced for just a moment about the simple things in life. He remembered when he and Tiff were about Ryan's age and how much joy he had around just getting pizza with the family. They didn't have much money when he was growing up, but it didn't seem to matter that much. Sure, they might not have had a lot of new clothes, the latest toys, or money to eat out often, but that didn't matter back then. The simple joys of childhood! As Ryan continued reenacting some of the week's biggest events, Thomas realized how much he had let things take precedence over people. But this was changing. Something had started to shift in the way he saw the world over the last few months. He grabbed another slice of pizza and gave Ryan a high five as Ryan completed the story of his sliding catch. Oh, to be six again! Thomas laughed for a moment, thinking that he and Tiff were probably almost as strapped for cash at this moment as their parents had been throughout their childhood.

This realization would have bothered Thomas significantly not long ago, but tonight it did not.

Thomas wondered if his world view was really changing. If so, why? And was it a change for the better? He definitely felt like he was seeing things differently but couldn't pinpoint exactly how or why this was happening. What was the big change? Was it this new role, directing the baseball camp? Maybe. Then he thought about the quote that he and Tiff were both drawn to. He had read through the list of quotes at least a dozen times over the last week. *Will you let it affect you?* That was the answer. It was simple, but he immediately knew that it was true. He was starting to let what Tiff had phrased "*wisdom distilled*" affect his thought process. It was similar to the way he had always let the ideas of successful entrepreneurs affect his thinking, infiltrate his daily life. Only now, the ideas affecting him had more wisdom, contained more truth. He wasn't just reading the words, or memorizing a bunch of quotes, he was pondering their implications and measuring them against many daily scenarios. He thought back to the first quote that he had highlighted on Tiff's papers:

"I can't imagine a man really enjoying a book and reading it only once."

He had really taken this to heart, even slowly and deliberately re-reading several chapters from the Narnia books late into the night. Ironically, even though he was now looking for wisdom, he was still rather surprised to find it popping up so regularly when he revisited the children's stories.

Tiff didn't interrupt her brother. She could clearly see that he was having a conversation with himself right there, in the booth at the pizzeria. She was also aware that the conversation seemed to be going well, and was having a positive effect on Thomas. Ryan, on the other hand, didn't mind interrupting at all, especially with something so important as baseball, ice cream, or both!

"Uncle Tommy, can we show mommy how good I hit the ball? If you eat all your pizza and, umm... if you pitch good, I'll make you an ice cream cone at home. Mommy, do we have ice cream?"

This little guy had it all worked out, but Tiff shook her head. With the bills still piling up and her meager income, she had been skimping on the groceries.

Uncle Tommy came to the rescue. "Good idea, buddy! How about this.... Let's go hit at the park right after we finish the pizza. Then we can pick up a carton of ice cream on the way home. My treat."

The boy had about the biggest grin imaginable pasted across his face at Thomas described this perfect ending to what Ryan considered a perfect week.

When they arrived at the park, it was quite busy, but the baseball field was empty. Thomas remembered baseball fields always being occupied when he was a kid. Was this accurate or just a result of classic rose-tinted memory? He was sure that it was accurate. Either way, the three of them grabbed some equipment from the trunk and took the field. Tiff would use Ryan's glove while her aspiring major leaguer batted.

"Bring it, Uncle Tommy!" Ryan shouted as he danced around in the batter's box, and then added in a quiet voice so his mother might not hear, "But not too fast."

Thomas stared in at the imaginary catcher and went into an exaggerated windup. Ryan hit practically every pitch hard and looked about as proud as a sweaty six-year-old with a sideways hat can look. Tiff did a much better job cheering than fielding the ball. After a few dozen hits, Tiff got Thomas' attention and tapped her wrist as if to say look at the time, it's almost time to get going. Ryan really got a hold of the next pitch, and sent it soaring into the outfield. The three went to collect the baseballs and Tiff said, "Just one more round, okay guys?"

Thomas walked through the outfield, his eyes scanning back and forth across the grass searching for baseballs. He was out in left field, searching for the last few balls, when his search was interrupted by a distant, but loud and familiar voice.

"Coach Thomas! Coach Thomas! Hey coach! Can I play, too?"

Thomas spun around, trying to locate the voice. He instantly knew that it was one of the players from camp. Of course, it had to be one of the campers. Who else would know him as coach? He saw a boy running towards him from the playground, with a woman following behind. Joey. And Clara.

Thomas had not seen Clara since the first morning that Joey joined the camp. Clara dropped him off for camp early that Monday but had made other driving arrangements for the rest of the week. Her work schedule started earlier and ended later than the camp. Each morning and evening that week, Thomas had hoped to see her, and was thrilled that his sister would finally get to meet Joey and Clara.

Thomas looked towards Tiff and Ryan, who were standing together next to home plate. It looked like Ryan was showing his mom one of the hitting drills, but was having a difficult time explaining to Tiff how to do her part to make the drill work. Thomas loved seeing his little protégé in action and he called to them, "Tiff! Ryan! It looks like we have another player... I mean two more players." Joey ran towards home plate and his mom ambled a few yards behind. Thomas realized that he had no idea if Clara would want to play, and suddenly remembered that Tiff was ready to head home.

By the time Thomas gathered the last few baseballs and reached home plate, the two mothers were chatting away. They had introduced themselves and their sons were now demonstrating the drill that Ryan had been struggling to explain. Tiff looked up at Thomas and announced, "It looks like we're ready for a game. Boys against girls. Thomas, the girls would like you to be the full-time pitcher."

Ryan and Joey looked up from their drill with the most shocked expressions. "Whoa! Yes!" they said, practically in unison. Thomas took the pitcher's mound, suggested places for the two moms to play in the field, and the game was on.

They played five innings and the boys won. It was close, but the moms' defense left a little to be desired. Thomas had to admit, Clara looked great in her son's hat. After a brief celebration, Joey announced that they could have a rematch another time. Both moms agreed, and everyone headed home for the night. Thomas realized that he didn't really get to talk to Clara very much that evening, but was pleased to see how much more confident and outgoing Joey had become over the last five days.

With the game over, it was time to say goodnight. Thomas thought it had been a full week, but had no idea of the reality check he was about to get from his sister.

How does She do it?

"Thomas, can I ask you something?" They were back in Tiff's apartment now. Ryan was asleep, and Thomas had just left his room to join Tiff in the backyard. It was a beautifully clear night. Warm, but not hot. A very slight breeze carried the smells of early summer – cut grass, flowers starting to bloom, nature bursting with life.

"Sure." Thomas thought it odd that Tiff would ask permission to ask a question and he added, "What else am I going to say? No, you may not ask me a question?"

"Okay, wise guy. Now that's the Thomas I know!" She shot him a sarcastic look that he knew was just in fun.

"Please do ask your question, dearest sister." He could certainly play the sarcasm game, if that's where she was going.

"Thomas, the experiment – remember that experiment that you started on the advice of your friend... friends, Joseph... and... Paul?" Tiff still found it difficult to say her late husband's name.

Thomas nodded, "Uh huh."

She took a few deep breaths to collect herself. "Are you... I mean, how is it going?" There was a genuine look of concern and interest on her face.

"Yeah," Thomas replied, "good question. Honestly, Tiff, I've been too busy. I guess it's like that old apple a day thing. Easy to do and easy not to do. For a few weeks, I was consistent. I would take a few minutes each morning to pray. Quietly and purposefully pray. Most of the time, I would do what Paul recommended. I'd pray about things I was thankful for. But really, since I've been so caught up in building and running the camp, I just haven't had the time. It's no big deal." Thomas paused, and for just a moment wondered if he had just made up an intricate and lame excuse. He continued, "I'll give it another go when I've got a bit more time."

"Oh, I see." That was all Tiff said before standing up. As she walked into the kitchen to get two glasses of water, she stopped right next to Thomas, looked him in the eyes, and said, "An apple a day matters. It *matters*."

Tiff seemed to take longer than usual getting the water. She was gathering her courage to continue the conversation. She wasn't sure how Thomas was going to respond.

When she finally did return, Thomas was standing up and holding his car keys. Tiff had a decision to make. This conversation was one that she knew would help him. But it was rather appealing to put it off for another day. *How often we do just that with important things,* she thought. *Wasn't it ironic that she was about to put off a conversation about putting off something that is very important?*

Thomas spoke first. "I've got to get going. Long week."

"Thomas – just a few minutes, please?" She had worked up the courage to address her brother. But, as soon as the words left her mouth, she realized that a few minutes might do more harm than good. The topic needed more than a few minutes.

Thomas just stood there, and she could tell he was weighing something in his mind. She was right. As Thomas stood there, he thought about what Tiff had done just a few hours ago at the park for him. It had been time to go home when Joey and Clara had arrived, yet Tiff didn't complain about playing a five-inning game. Although he was tired and anticipating a full weekend, he slowly sat back down. He owed his little sister.

She decided to get right to the point. "Thomas, what I mean is – I can see a difference. I see it in you and I feel it in me. You're different when you have that little habit in your days. You're more … patient, focused – well maybe you're always pretty focused, but you seem more focused on what really matters – you're more understanding, better with Ryan, more humble, a better communicator. Thomas, I see these things, as clear as night and day. I could tell the difference without you telling me. I knew you hadn't made time to pray each day for the last week or so." She

I Once Was Lost

looked up at her brother and was pleasantly surprised to see that he was looking back at her, silently nodding in agreement. She decided to continue, to make sure he knew how important this was. "At the baseball field tonight, Thomas, you were really impatient with Ryan about throwing the balls back out to you – and with the way you criticized him for having to be reminded to hunt down the foul balls. And Ryan told me that you *'talk mad'* to the coaches sometimes during camp." She knew these statements would typically get under Thomas' skin, so she braced herself before looking over at her brother. The defensive posture she expected was exactly what she saw.

Thomas was okay with the beginning of Tiff's discussion, but this was over the line. She didn't understand what he was trying to do. She didn't understand the importance of setting the bar high and holding the line. Otherwise people would walk all over you. And that includes assistant coaches as well as first-graders, even if they are – especially if they are – your nephew or son. Tiff needed to be set straight. Thomas shook his head dismissively and with a hint of condescension.

"Tiff..." As he heard his own voice saying his sister's name, he was shocked by the blatantly patronizing tone. He tried again, without much improvement. "Tiff, I hear you, but you're wrong. What do you want me to do, just let the assistant coaches be lazy? Or teach my nephew that it's okay to not try your hardest? Tiff, this is the real world here."

"Thomas!" She blurted out his name very abruptly, cutting short what seemed like it might turn into a lecture she had heard before. "Thomas, please just stop for a second!"

"Okay, go ahead." He said the words but didn't want her input. Not right now. His tone communicated as much.

Tiff was doubting whether she would be able to make the point she was trying to make without just creating resentment. She didn't know the answer and concluded that it might be best to just admit that. "I'm not sure what the best way is. But what if you brought that to your prayer time? I guess what I'm saying is bring the question to your prayer, a question that sounds something like this: 'I'm trying to teach Ryan and my assistant coaches to be responsible, to have high standards, to take initiative. What is the best way – or a better way than I've been using?' Thomas, I don't think I have all the answers here. But would it hurt to try that?"

Thomas was surprised to find himself nodding his head in agreement. One thing he knew for sure, and his sister had the guts to call him on it – his way wasn't working all that well. "Yeah. I think it's worth a try."

They sat together in silence for a few long seconds before Thomas got up and grabbed his car keys.

"Goodnight, Tiff," he said as he walked towards the front door. Pausing before closing the door, he looked back and almost whispered, "And thank you." He meant these words.

Easier Said than Done

Monday morning marked the beginning of baseball camp week three. Thomas was so ready to go. For the last three days, he had not only made time for daily prayer – particularly talking with God about how best to both connect with and challenge his assistants and the campers – but he had also made a little corner of his house into a place for his daily prayer. Having a designated place made it stand out a little more. He respected Tiff for challenging him to do this and had a renewed resolve to make it stick. He even printed a quote that he found online and taped it to his car's dashboard. It was from Corrie Ten Boom, the famous Nazi concentration camp survivor and author of *The Hiding Place*. Her words were simple and clear.

"Do not pray when you feel like it. Have an appointment with the Lord and keep it."

Thomas even made a note to himself to read her book.

He went to Tiff's house early that morning to pick up Ryan, but he also had something to ask his sister.

She had to get to work and there wasn't much time to talk, so he asked, "There's a situation I would love some help thinking through. Can I give you a quick overview and then maybe we can discuss it when we have some time?"

"Sure," Tiff was grabbing her things and about to walk out the front door. "But make it quick!"

He followed her towards the door. "Tiff, about that assistant coach that Ryan said I talk mean to... there may be some truth to Ryan's assessment. I've been wanting to talk to you about that. I have this assistant coach – something has to be done about him, his name is Ben. He's one of those guys with a massive chip on his shoulder. He brings an attitude to almost everything he does, and the attitude is affecting some of the other coaches and campers. I've had a couple interactions with him, but he's not really showing any improvement. It's really time to straighten this out. And I guess, in line with what you just brought up a few nights ago, I've been putting it off because I know that I need an effective way to have this conversation."

By this point, they were standing next to Tiff's car and she really had to get going. But, instead of rushing off immediately, Tiff looked at Thomas with empathy. She had crossed paths with many a person with a difficult attitude – that needed *straightening out*. In some ways, she thought to herself, Thomas was having to deal with *himself* in more ways than one. She didn't have an easy answer for him. In fact, it was something she didn't think she really knew how to handle. But she also knew it was something that had to be handled. One bad attitude can have too much of a negative impact on the group – it's like one rotten apple in a basket of apples. Pretty soon the bad one causes all the good apples to rot.

"I know what you're saying, Thomas. Trust me, I know. And you're right, something does need to be done. And soon." Tiff sat down in the driver's seat. She spoke slowly, thinking through what she thought might work in the situation. Then, suddenly her eyes lit up. "Thomas, what if you brought that to your prayer every day over the next week before having a formal conversation with Ben?"

"Hmmm," was Thomas' response. "Yeah, I guess I didn't really think about that. I can't just ignore it, but I can certainly make it part of the daily prayer. That's going really well, by the way. At least for the last three days."

"Awesome! Okay, my brother, I really have to go." She waved out the window as she drove away, calling out, "Bye! Ryan, have fun today. Mommy loves you so much!"

An Unexpected Message

"There are only two types of people in this game: those who have been humbled by the game and those who will be. The game is baseball. And the game is life."

The words were printed on a small note inside an envelope with that was plainly labeled, *"Coach Thomas"* and nothing more. No signature, no date. It was clearly meant for him, but from whom? Two types of people, thought Thomas. Sure. Among his first thoughts: thanks for pointing out the obvious. But much of his recent experience reminded him that the obvious isn't always all that obvious. Even more rare: living the wisdom that we already think we know. Baseball certainly had a way of humbling people. I guess life does, too, he thought. What is this anonymous person trying to say? Which does this person think I am? He had to assume the person was saying that he, Coach Thomas, needed to be humbled. But maybe there was more to the note. He checked the time and realized that he was still very early and could take a few minutes out to reflect. He sent Ryan on an errand to set up one of the stations and sat down on the bench in the dugout. This prayer thing was growing on him. He wasn't completely comfortable with it yet, and still often felt like he was just talking to himself. But, he had to admit that his little sister was right. When it was part of his day, it made a significant difference.

Now he sat in the dugout and talked to God – and to himself – about the anonymous note. It was taking a little getting used to, but he even used phrases now and again in his silent dialogue, phrases like, "God, what do you think of this? God, what does this mean? God, what am I supposed to do here?" He wasn't sure if he was supposed to expect an answer, and still got distracted in his own inner conversation more often than not, but it felt right. It was a lot like what Tiff had described as the truth sounding sweet to the ears. Praying in this way, quietly asking God for an answer, help, guidance. He wasn't about to try to explain it to anyone else, but it did have that sweet to the ears feeling.

Ryan was about fifty yards away, busily setting up a station. The assistant coaches had not yet arrived on this morning. So there Thomas sat, in silence. His worked his way around to his question this morning. "God, have I been humbled, or do I need to be humbled? What do I need to learn here?" With his eyes still closed for a few peaceful seconds, he asked, "God, is this a lesson that I need in baseball or life – or both?"

He sat upright and opened his eyes. *It's both.* The idea was suddenly crystal clear in his mind. "It's both. It's always both." Without even realizing it, he had said this aloud. *It's simple*, he thought. *I both have been humbled and continually need to be humbled in both baseball and life.* He closed his eyes once more and, this time, he rested his chin on his folded hands. It made so much sense, but then it didn't. What about confidence? So many experiences had reinforced Thomas' belief that success goes to the confident, in baseball and life. Confident and humble? Could this be both as well? He was thinking about it and decided to ask God about this one, as well. *God, is this another both? Help me out here!*

"Morning Coach!" Willie's loud and jovial voice interrupted the peaceful moment. "Aw, coach, I'm sorry. I didn't mean to wake you up. Beauty sleep's so important, especially when you start getting older." This kid was too much. The early group had just arrived and there were more of them this week than there had been the previous week. They were all laughing at Willie's comment and Thomas silently hoped that no one had seen the coach talking to himself. He preferred the idea of the coach getting beauty sleep to that of a head coach who talked to himself. Then it hit him. So what if they thought he was talking to himself? And what if they knew he was starting his day in prayer? What if they knew their coach was praying? For some reason, that wasn't considered okay?

Why did he feel self-conscious about his players thinking that he prayed? This bothered Thomas. He wasn't one to worry much about what others thought, but the prayer thing… what was it about that? Strange. He had no problem telling players to talk to themselves when they were pitching, hitting, or fielding. He'd use expressions like, "You got this. You got this. Hard hit ground ball, I'm going to second." Or "Bat to the ball. Bat to the ball. See it, hit it. Just see it, hit it."

Thomas walked towards the outfield and pondered this. Why was he hung up on the players knowing that he was praying? That he was talking to God about baseball? That he was asking God for input, for guidance, for help? This question still perplexed Thomas as the campers started to arrive and baseball camp week three was underway.

A Date?

By Thursday afternoon, Thomas was ready for a break. All in all, the week was going well. Sure, there had been a few interactions with the assistant coaching staff that didn't go perfectly, but the improvements he had mapped out after the first week and then tweaked a little more after week two were working out very well. The thing that bothered him most this week was the dipping energy level of many of the assistant coaches. And, of course, there were a few run-ins with Ben. He wasn't certain that these interactions were going well, and certainly didn't see any improvement in Ben's behavior or attitude. Keeping his promise to Tiff, Thomas was bringing the best ways to handle interactions with Ben to his daily morning prayer. He felt a lot better about it but was still searching for that "wisdom distilled" answer to appear!

The parents started arriving for pickup and Thomas was busily conversing with a few parents about their children's progress when Tiff pulled into the parking lot. Thomas didn't see her pull in and, as far as she knew, he was completely unaware of her plan. She fully intended to keep it that way. In truth, it wasn't much of a plan. It was more of a hopeful idea that might work out the way she imagined and, either way, she figured it was worth a try. Ryan saw her right away and called out in a loud and excited voice, "Mommy!!! Mommy! Come see what I can do! Mom!!" She heard him on the first call and was heading over to see her proud son in his filthy baseball uniform. Ryan proceeded to show his mother just about every drill and game they had worked on throughout the camp. He also pointed out the various other players that had become his new friends. What a great age, Tiff thought. Not yet old enough to be too cool to give his Mom a tour, her little boy was a sponge. From the way he talked, she could practically see him running the whole camp. He knew why the drills were run a certain way, knew the purpose of various exercises, throwing motions, footwork, fielding positions. Tiff tried to remember if she knew this much about any sport when she was his age. Ryan's excitement to show her everything fit perfectly into her plan. This would take up some time.

Thomas was surprised to see her when he glanced over during his conversation with several parents. He waved to his sister and wrinkled his forehead as if to say, "what are you doing here?" He didn't know she would be picking up Ryan that afternoon.

When the parents Thomas had been speaking with went to gather their children, Tiff called over, "I got out of work a little early today and thought I'd check in on you... I keep hearing how amazing this baseball camp is and wanted to see for myself! Looks like the staff here really know what they're doing." She was only able to look over at Thomas for a moment, as Ryan was now leading her on to the next fielding station.

Thomas went back to his daily wrap-up routine but found himself smiling every few minutes when he would hear a very familiar "Come on, Mommy!" followed by compassionate and truly excited interjections from his sister. "Wow, Ryan, this is amazing!" and "How do you know all this?" Tiff disguised her frequent glances towards the parking lot, hoping that Thomas wouldn't notice, hoping her plan just might work out. The minutes passed and most of the campers had departed. Including Ryan, there were only five kids left when Thomas heard Joey's voice, about as excited as he had heard it. When Thomas walked around the dugout, he saw the reason. Clara was jogging towards her little ballplayer. Joey sprinted towards her and she almost lost her balance as he gave her a monstrous running hug. So much for her clean work outfit! Clara didn't even seem phased by the dirt that transferred from Joey's clothing to hers. Thomas stopped walking and just watched the interaction. Just like his own mother, he thought. She loved hugs and a little dirty clothing didn't seem to bother her in the slightest. When Clara looked over at Thomas, he put his hand up and said, "Hi there! Fancy seeing you at the ballfield." This was the first time Clara had picked up Joey after camp. She had dropped him off that first day and on a few other days, but had rushed off to make it to work on time. Her work schedule didn't allow much extra time and Thomas could certainly appreciate that.

By this point, Tiff walked over to Clara and the two hugged like old friends. How does that work, Thomas wondered? They had only met one time, but now they were practically kindred spirits, long-lost friends. Maybe it's a mother thing. Thomas knew that there are some things you just don't figure out.

Tiff and Clara were chatting away, while Thomas and the assistant coaches finished getting everything wrapped up for the day and the last remaining campers were picked up. By the time Thomas walked over to formally say hello, he overheard his sister say, "Great. We'll see you at my place when you get there. No hurry. I'll make some food for the boys and I'm sure they're going to have so much fun playing." Tiff turned and called Ryan and Joey to get into her car. As they loaded in, she off-handedly mentioned to Thomas that the boys were coming to her house to play for a while. Tiff got into her can. Ryan and Joey were in the back seat, and then, as if she had almost forgotten, she called out the window to Thomas, "Oh, I told Clara maybe you could drive her to the grocery store and then swing by my place after. No rush. She can leave her car here and we'll get her back here later." Tiff was driving away before Thomas had time to comprehend or question the logistics she had outlined.

The field was completely empty except for Clara and Thomas. They both found themselves slightly dazed, as if they had missed some part of the plan. In a way, the setting was perfect. They were on a college baseball field and feeling a bit like the first day of college. I have to be where? When? And how, exactly do I get there? Did I sign up for this?

Clara looked at Thomas with a small laugh. "I do need a few groceries and was going to take Joey with me, but your sister offered to take the kids to her place. She said something about it being easier to have you give me a ride to her place than trying to explain directions. We can..."

Thomas butted in, "Let's take my car. I need a few things at the store, anyway." The two got into Thomas' convertible. It was a pleasantly warm evening, but not too hot – the kind of weather convertibles are built for. By the time they drove away, Tiff's car was out sight, and she could only hope that her plan was working. If only she knew how well it was going to work...

They were almost done at the grocery store when Thomas got a text message from his sister. "No rush. Boys having so much fun." He messaged back, "Done @ store. Be there in a few." Tiff came right back with, "No." and then, "Can you be an awesome brother and get me a bag of those amazingly rich coffee beans from the Café in town?" Thomas thought, *Why not?* They put their groceries in the trunk and he mentioned they'd need to make one more quick stop. The café, it turned out, wouldn't be as quick a stop as anticipated. Thomas knew exactly which coffee beans Tiff meant. For special occasions, he would often get her a roast that the café made themselves. She didn't drink coffee often, but when she did, she absolutely loved the richness of that bean. As luck would have it, the café happened to be roasting a new batch when they arrived. They would have to wait a few minutes, but would get a fresh bag of coffee beans. The café owner kindly suggested that they enjoy a freshly brewed iced coffee while they wait. Clara initially shook her head slightly to decline, but Thomas made a well-known Italian gesture for delicious, ordered two, and said, "My treat. If you don't love it, I guess I'll have to drink two." They found two very comfortable chairs in the lounge space by the window. Clara sat back and appeared to be relaxed for the first time that afternoon. It looked to Thomas like she might not have taken a deep breath in weeks.

"Thomas, this is absolutely delicious. Thank you!"

"Did you doubt?" He smiled. "Clara, we can relax for a few minutes. Tiff just texted me that the kids are having a blast. No hurry. Besides, the coffee roasting will take some time."

Clara raised her glass, slowly took another sip, shook her head and said, "Mmmmm Ummmm."

Thomas appreciated the way she could enjoy such a simple thing as a cup of coffee. Her words at their first meeting came back to his mind, although they had not been far from his thoughts for very long in the months that had passed. "A wise person once told me that 'Life is what you make it.' I wish I could say that I live that expression, but I am making some progress."

Clara laughed and Thomas continued, "You weren't kidding, your son really loves to play baseball."

"Yes, he does." Clara settled into the big comfortable chair and looked out the café's large front window. Her heart was full of gratitude for the chance to see her son at camp earlier that evening. With her crazy work schedule and trying to just keep everything together, she often felt that she was missing too many important things in his life. She so rarely made time for anything but work and Joey. Sometimes she felt torn about this. She knew that her son needed her, but also knew how important it was to recharge her own batteries. There simply was not enough time in the day.

She came back to the present, realizing that she had no idea how long she had been looking out the window. She was relieved to see that Thomas was looking kindly at her, and didn't seem to be impatient or uncomfortable in the prolonged silence.

She finally broke the silence, "Thomas, I like it – your expression. It sounds good, but I'm not so sure. It's so much easier to say that than to live it."

Thomas had an idea, but hesitated to share his thought with Clara. He chose not to speak and just nodded in agreement. He put his right hand on his pocket and felt that the well-worn papers with quotes from Tiff were still there.

Clara breathed in through her nose to capture the aroma of the roasting coffee beans. "I can understand why your sister likes that coffee so much. What a great smell." Was she trying to change the subject? "You've got a good sister, Thomas. You are very blessed to have her in your life."

Thomas knew that. "Yeah, she's a special woman." He wasn't at all surprised that Clara and Tiff seemed to hit it off so quickly. They both had such an amazing quality – an authenticity. *Authenticity* – yes, that was the best word Thomas could come up with to describe these two women.

She returned to the original subject. "I wish I could say that I live that expression, Thomas. It's real, but so many things get in the way. Lately, I feel like the world is making my life more than I am." She sounded a bit sad and Thomas really wished he knew if it would be best to inquire further, to share his own struggles, or to default back to his standard response when things got too deep: say something funny to lighten the moment.

"Me too." He was surprised when the words came out of his mouth. This was not like him. "Well what I mean…" he was struggling to decide if he should go back to making a joke or continue down the rabbit hole and into the unknown world of sharing something he didn't feel he could control. Down the rabbit hole he tumbled. "I guess I – um – I've been questioning a lot of things lately. It's… strange… yes, that's probably the best word for it – strange. It's strange. On one hand I have this sense of peace about these new jobs. On the other hand, I feel a bit like things are just happening to me. And in the process, I've ended up questioning almost everything I've built my life around. I feel lost…" He couldn't believe that he had just said all this, especially those last words about feeling lost. He didn't really know Clara that well. Okay, he felt like he knew her well, but they had only really shared a few conversations. Telling her he felt lost – how did that slip out? In a way, what he had just said aloud was an example of what he was trying – struggling, really – to explain. Later that night he would wonder why he allowed himself to keep speaking, but he went on. "Yeah, lost." With a small, mysterious smile, he added, "And I feel found."

"Thomas," Clara was laughing gently, but not at him. She clearly found something funny and just had to share it with him now, even if it meant butting in on what he would later that night consider his therapy session. "You're lost and found. I love it!" He didn't realize that he had practically identified himself in this way. The way she said it, he burst out laughing, too.

"I guess I am. We need a sign: 'Lost and Found.' Right here."

The two talked and sipped their delicious coffee for what seemed like half an hour or more, until Thomas suddenly noticed that the bag of coffee he had requested was sitting on the small table in front of him. The café owner must have placed it there without their notice. He felt her hand touch his arm as she said, "We can make the delivery to your sister now." They locked eyes for a moment and Thomas could see something in her eyes that simultaneously comforted him and made him feel slightly uncomfortable. *What was it?* He wondered.

On the drive to Tiff's house, the aroma of freshly roasted coffee mixing with the fresh evening air overpowered one's sense of smell. The conversation turned to the camp and Joey's excitement over every little lesson and happening of the days. Thomas truly appreciated hearing all of this from Clara, as he so often would get lost in attempts to make the camp great without stepping back and allowing himself to be moved by a single child's experience.

When they arrived at Tiff's house, the boys were so involved with playing in the backyard that they didn't even take notice. Tiff was in the kitchen, putting the final touches on a pasta and salad dinner. She motioned for them to have a seat, saying in her best hostess accent, "Kindly do take a seat. Your dinner is served."

Clara placed the bag of freshly roasted coffee beans on the counter. She really liked the warm and fun atmosphere and was so grateful to be there. Joey and Ryan were throwing a tennis ball against the back of the building. Apparently, they had made their own version of baseball camp and were taking turns creating activities. The boys' faces said it all. They would not want this play time to come to an end. Clara took a seat, her eyes shifted upwards, towards the ceiling, and she mouthed the words, "Thank you," before closing her eyes for a few seconds.

Tiff called the kids for dinner. When they were all seated together, Joey looked at his mother, pulled his head close to hers, and quietly whispered something in her ear. Then he pulled his head away and looked at her for a reply. With a smile and a slight nod, she said, "Yes. Of course." Then she turned to Tiff and said, "We always say a quick thank you prayer before we eat. Joey wanted to know if we would do that here, too. May I?"

Clara reached out her hand and Joey took it in his. When they did this, Ryan was seated on the other side of Joey and just naturally reached out to hold Joey's other hand. Kids so often have a way of making unnecessarily complicated things simple. Ryan took his mother's hand with his free hand, prompting Tiff and Thomas to complete the circle back to Clara. Clara was pleasantly surprised as she patiently watched this unfold. Joey had her left hand and now Thomas had her right hand. She bowed her head and spoke just a few heartfelt and genuine words of thanks before they shared a very basic but wonderful meal together.

The rest of the evening passed by too quickly, filled with much laughter and pleasant conversation. After Thomas dropped Joey and Clara off at her car by the baseball field, he drove back to Tiff's house to keep his promise of reading to Ryan every evening at bed time. On the drive, he tried to remember the words Clara had used in her prayer of thanks. It was simple, beautiful, and relevant. It went something like this:

"God, thank you. [extended pause] Thank you for the gift of food and wonderful people to share it with. You remind us of what matters most. Help us to give our time and focus accordingly. We have so much to be thankful for. Amen."

As he tried to recall the words, he wasn't sure if she had said a bit more than this or a bit less. The thing that struck him most was the feeling that went with her words. What was the emotion he had felt as she spoke? Was it her emotion or his? He parked in front of Tiff's house, shut the car off, and just sat in silence, pondering. Suddenly, the answer occurred to him. The emotion he felt as she had prayed was a mix of pure gratitude and humility. It was hers, but became his as she spoke. Of course. Humble gratitude. If that could be bottled, and put on display, this woman had just done it. He jumped out of the car with that hop in your step you have when you've just solved something big.

Ryan was in his pajamas and ready to read, but first had an announcement. "Uncle Tommy, Joey would like Narnia. Could we lend him some of my books?"

"You bet we can, buddy." Thomas was so proud of this little guy. He sat on the chair by Ryan's bed and reflected briefly on the thought that maybe kids are in our lives so that we can learn from them, too, not just the other way around. "Humble gratitude," he said to himself.

"What did you say, Uncle Tommy?" Apparently, Thomas had said the words loud enough for Ryan to hear.

"I said 'humble gratitude, buddy.'" Ryan looked at him with inquisitive eyes, so Thomas tried to explain. "I guess it means when you are really happy to have something in your life, even though you know you couldn't really earn it. Like you, buddy!" Thomas was trying to both explain it to Ryan and clarify his own understanding at the same time. "What could I possible do to deserve to have such an awesome nephew? Humble gratitude. Being thankful for everything – and everyone – in your life. Does that make any sense?"

Ryan let the idea sink in and Thomas could see that his gears were turning. Thomas knew he hadn't done a great job in trying to explain the concept, but, to be honest, he realized that just a few months ago, he probably would not have even tried. He likely wouldn't even have put those two words together. *Humble gratitude.*

"Uncle Tommy, the neighbor brought my kickball back to me. I didn't even know that it was in her yard. When she brought it back, I was so happy! Is it like that? She could've kept it and played with it. But she didn't. She brought it back to me. And I thanked her a bunch of times. Is that 'humble ...' – what did you call it?"

"Humble gratitude. Yeah. I like that. That's a good example, Ryan."

They shared a quick fist bump to celebrate the accomplishment before Ryan moved on and said, "Okay, let's read!"

Thomas picked up the book and the two drifted further into another adventure in Narnia with Jill Pole and Eustace Scrub. Lately, it was becoming more and more difficult for Thomas to stop reading when Ryan was finally asleep. Instead of reading ahead, Thomas had resorted to re-reading some of the books they had already read. On the second time reading, he even took a few notes on his phone as he went. Several things captured his attention, but tonight one consistent theme jumped out. It was a theme he may have noticed during their first read, but now it was louder and clearer than before.

The books spoke directly to him, directly to his current reality, to his challenges. The stories and words comforted him and challenged him. There was more of what he had begun to call *"distilled wisdom"* in these fairy tales than he had noticed – or expected – before. And he was soaking it up on the second read. Aslan knew what was going on, in his wisdom, and even called people out when appropriate. They couldn't lie to him. Aslan knew. He didn't let them off easy. One of Aslan's phrases from the Magician's Nephew caught Thomas off guard.

"Oh, Adam's sons, how cleverly you defend yourselves against all that might do you good!"

Thomas shuddered as he spoke the words into the notepad on his phone. He didn't want to think about the amount of effort he, himself, had made throughout his life to resist choices that would have done him good. He was still sitting in the chair by Ryan's bed, reading under small lamp while Ryan slept peacefully. Tiff heard her brother read these words, as she was now standing in the doorway gazing at her little sleeping angel.

"Thomas, what are you doing?" she asked softly. "Are you talking to yourself?"

He looked up in surprise. "Oh, hey sis. I'm just taking my beating like a man." He laughed as they walked together into the kitchen.

"Taking your beating? What in the world are you talking about?" She couldn't remember hearing her brother say something like that before.

"Well, Tiff, do you remember that note about being humbled by the game – or by life – I've been re-reading some of the Narnia books with the mindset of *'There's some lesson in there for my life.'* In a way, I am asking the question *'How should this story affect me?'* and *'How should it humble me?'*"

Tiff turned towards her brother, then suddenly grabbed his shoulders firmly with both of her hands and firmly pulled him closer to her. She stared into his eyes intensely and demanded, "Who are you? And what have you done with my brother?" Pleased with making her point in such a theatrical manner, a look of a satisfied motherly figure swept across her face.

"Tiff, I'm serious here."

"So am I," she shot back.

"Tiff," he continued, "I actually told Clara tonight – when we were at the café – that I was both lost and found. I told her I felt more lost in life than I ever have. Tiff, I'm looking for answers. I don't know how I got here, but I've started searching for answers as if they are out there and I might not have any of them."

Tiff nodded and replied, "Thomas, I don't think you're as lost as you might think. I think you were more lost before you realized that you were lost. I don't know how to explain this, but I see you. You. I mean, I see who you really are coming out more and more. You're still Thomas, but you're so much less impatient. You have more fun. Sure, you're still a pain in the neck on a fairly regular basis, but it's different. You're different." Tiff's voice trailed off.

Thomas quietly absorbed what his sister was saying before she continued, "Thomas, I meant it. What is going on with you? It's great, but I – well, I'm worried. I'm not worried about the way you've been. I'm worried that it won't last. Ryan needs this version of you in his life. But it's more than that. That's my selfish reason. It's so much more than that. The kids in this baseball camp need this version of you in their lives." Her eyes had become moist as she spoke, and Thomas saw a single tear trickle down her cheek.

Thomas didn't know what to say. Instead, they both just sat together in silence. Somehow, it's only possible to sit comfortably in silence with another person if you don't know them at all, or if you know them so well that neither is expecting something from the other. Eventually, they said their goodbyes and Thomas headed home.

Easy is not an Option

Thomas' surprise the next morning was less than pleasant. Well after camp was underway, two of the assistant coaches were still missing. Without any notice, Ben and one of his buddies had not shown up. After getting the camp underway, Thomas filled in at one of the stations that didn't require much interaction from the coach to keep things on track and sent a few text messages to the missing parties. There was no response as the minutes passed. Thomas knew that they needed at least one of these coaches to show up to have the right coach to camper ratio, and he didn't have any luck getting in touch with a fill-in. In addition to having the right ratios, Thomas was not happy that several of the programs planned for the day would not be as effective if they were missing two of the staff. Finally, a reply came in the form of a text, but it was not the reply Thomas wanted.

"Not going to make it today." It came from Ben.

Thomas' knee-jerk reaction was to send a scathing reply, in caps. Something like: "UNACCEPTABLE. U need to get here NOW." He wrote it and hit send. No response. Thomas was fuming. Ben definitely got the message. What was his deal? What excuse would he have? Was he working on an excuse or just playing one of his games? Thomas' anger grew as he pictured Ben's smug expression with an *I'll respond when I get around to it* attitude. He checked his phone again and thought about the next message he would send. By this point, he was walking – more like marching – down the right field line along the edge of the woods. His blood was boiling. The plan for this day required the entire staff and every single assistant coach knew it. He had made this abundantly clear more than once. Where were they? Before sending a follow up text, he called the other missing assistant, a more reserved young man named Josh, who had known Ben since grade school. Josh spent more time with Ben than Thomas liked, but didn't have the same edge that Ben

116

carried. Josh's phone rang several times before he answered, rather meekly, "Coach... ummm..."

Thomas knew an excuse was coming. It better be a good one, but he wouldn't buy any excuse at this point. He withheld his outburst for a few seconds, but his marching became more forceful and he imagined that Ben was right next to Josh. Thomas' jaw slanted and his nostrils flared with anger. Josh heard heavy breathing through the phone and knew that his boss and coach had good reason to be furious. Josh's words sounded weak. "Coach, it was – um – kind of last minute. Our friends – well, me and Ben – a few of our friends asked us to go to an amusement park with them today. We didn't really think..." Thomas cut him off.

"You're joking, right?" He fired at the young man. "This is a joke?"

Josh stammered but Thomas didn't allow a response.

"Tell me exactly where you are!"

"We're going to... I mean we're at..." Josh knew he was in the wrong and could feel his boss and new college baseball coach's anger.

"How far away? You need to get here immediately!" Thomas was about to tell Josh that both he and Ben need not waste anyone's time in even showing up for fall college baseball tryouts.

"Uh, coach it's maybe 4 or 5 hours. We left really early this morning. With traffic now, it's probably more than 5 hours to get back." Josh could only imagine how feeble this must sound to his new coach and wished he could go back and rethink the whole decision. He felt guilty, embarrassed, and most of all ashamed for letting himself be talked into doing something he knew was wrong.

Thomas said nothing for a few seconds, and then exploded. "That is unacceptable! You need to get here.! You knew the plans. You know the ratios. It's unacceptable. Do you hear me? Get here! NOW!" He hung up the phone and walked away from the field and into the woods. There was a brook that ran along the first base line just a few yards into the woods. Thomas picked up a smooth rock, a bit bigger than a baseball, and threw it full force at a tree. Whack! He threw several more rocks at that tree. By this point, he was mad at everyone. Ben. Josh. The other assistant coaches – surely some of them must have known what Ben and Josh had planned. He was angry with himself for not straightening Ben out days ago. How did he let this happen? He knew that Ben needed to be dealt with, yet he had let it go. Tiff. He was even angry with his sister. She had talked him into waiting to deal with Ben and now he was paying the price. Soft doesn't work. He fired another rock into the woods. Crack! Thomas needed to get back to the field. It was time to rotate stations and he would need to change some of the program for the day to make up for his two defectors. Who else knew? Was this just another test of the new coach? He turned away from the stream and started walking back to the field. He wasn't any less angry. If anything, he was even more infuriated now. His rage was directed at the whole world around him. Even at the college board for giving him this role. He wasn't a coach. He was clearly the wrong choice. Perhaps it was time to end the charade and go back to the real world, the world he knew, the world he could better control.

Thomas went to one of the activities that required two coaches and was being temporarily staffed by just one. He joined the activity, but his mind was not there. He was racking his brain for a solution. Five hours? Were Ben and Josh really that far away? He remembered going to the same amusement park in his teens. Yes, it was probably that long a trip, maybe more since they would be fighting summer beach traffic. Would they even come back today? If they did, he wasn't sure if he'd let them participate or simply fire them and send them home. Thomas didn't really speak to anyone for the next few hours. At lunch time, he sat alone with papers spread out in front of him, trying to finalize modifications of the afternoon mini competitions that originally needed the full staff. He had heard nothing from Ben or Josh. In a way, he almost hoped they would send an excuse text saying something like traffic was even worse than usual and they were going to be even later or explaining that they were the drivers for several friends and had to stay at the amusement park. He was ready to fire back a message telling them not to even bother coming back today, or for the rest of the summer. He would make this camp work, but his mind was entertaining thoughts of making an almost immediate return to the business world. Several recent emails and phone calls had brought options of joining or running another start-up. He didn't owe the college anything. This was a near impossible assignment they had given him. On top of everything else, the salary was ludicrous in comparison with the responsibilities, time investment, not to mention the aggravation of dealing with college kids. Yes, he thought, time to put an end to this foolish experiment.

The afternoon went okay, considering. A follow-up message from the two renegade coaches never arrived. Neither did they.

After camp, Thomas dropped Ryan off at Tiff's house and took a long drive on winding back roads. Tiff had stood in the doorway and simply nodded silently when he let her know he might not be back in time to read with Ryan that night. He shut off his phone and put the car in sport shift mode, letting the engine rev close to redline before advancing the gears. He tried to clear his mind, but it kept racing through everything, over and over. Driving fast on winding roads was his prescription for the evening. He was going but fast, but nowhere, with no intended destination. Finally, as the sun started to dip below the hills, he pulled the car off the road and got out to take in the incredible colors nature shared.

If there was one consistent and dominant thought that kept replaying in his mind that evening, it was simply this: "I'm not a coach. Who am I kidding? I'm a business guy, not a coach." Just a few weeks ago, a year had seemed like a very reasonable amount of time to give this new role a fair shot. Now, a year seemed like an eternal plunge into insanity. He didn't even want to imagine what other instances of immaturity an entire year would bring. Time to get out. Pull the plug on the experiment. That's what it was, he thought, nothing more than a failed experiment. He brought the situation back to his familiar business language. Sunk costs. Don't throw bad money after good. If a marketing strategy or a product aren't working, there comes a time to just abandon ship and move on.

It was late by the time Thomas made it back home. Tiff must have put Ryan to bed that evening. Thomas felt a twinge of regret for missing his commitment, but he was certain that Ryan and Tiff would understand.

The next morning brought a renewed conviction that Thomas had to do what was best for Thomas. Sure, the college might be a little upset. The board would have to resume their search. But Thomas had been clear about this with them. Several times he brought up the fact that his experience might not lend itself to the challenges of the new roles. He had some time to spare and decided to stop at the park by the river before heading on to camp. His was the only car in the parking lot, but there was a silhouette of a man on that familiar bench by the water. Could it be? No. Thomas rubbed his eyes and his heartbeat increased in anticipation. Yes! It had to be Joseph. He walked over to the big man, said hello, and was greeted by a giant bear hug and a rich, "Hello, my dear friend. Hello!"

Thomas just stood there in disbelief for a moment. Since his first meeting with Joseph at this same park, every trip to the park carried an expectancy, even a hope, that Joseph would be there again.

"Please do join me and take a seat, that is, if you have the time," came the warm invitation from Joseph.

Thomas sat down, but remained very aware of the time. He would need to leave shortly to get to camp.

"Tell me, Thomas, what troubles you?"

So much for small talk, Thomas thought. How did this man appear and somehow cut straight to the heart of things so quickly? What troubles me, Thomas wasn't sure if he repeated the question aloud or just in his own mind. That was some question. Where would he begin?

"I've got some challenges... but don't we all?" Thomas planned to keep this conversation very surface level, but that changed when Joseph just looked at him with a deep gaze that communicated, *"You can tell your troubles."*

As Thomas briefly recounted the events of the camp, Joseph just listened intently with an occasional nod, brief question, or word to encourage Thomas to continue describing the situation. It was comforting to get the whole story out there. Thomas didn't ask for advice or guidance, but secretly hoped the old man would agree with the decision Thomas had already reached. At the same time, Thomas was ready to counter the counsel he expected. In his mind, he could picture Joseph suggesting that he honor his commitment. The two sat quietly for many seconds and Joseph looked like he was about to do exactly what Thomas had anticipated. Thomas didn't let him. It was time to go get the camp day started, so he abruptly stood up just as Joseph's mouth opened to speak.

"Sorry, Joseph. I've got to go." Thomas was about to turn away when his friend stopped him.

"Thomas! Can I ask two favors of you?"

Thomas impatiently said, "Yes. Go ahead."

"The first: can we meet right here on Saturday morning? Same time?"

Thomas nodded. He was thrilled at the idea of knowing he'd see his friend again so soon.

"The second: What perspective would my good friend C.S. Lewis have for you in this current predicament? Could you bring your thoughts along for our discussion on Saturday morning?"

"Absolutely. You've got it. Joseph, I will see you soon... and, Thank you!" Thomas chirped the car's tires as he pulled out of the parking spot and headed for the field. There was much to be done before Saturday morning.

Saturday in the Park

A soft rain was falling on Saturday morning. Camp – and everything else leading up to Saturday morning – went by like a blur. Despite an incredibly full week, Thomas made the time to read with Ryan every day. He posted openings in preparation for replacing Ben and Josh. The two renegades, as he had come to call them, did show up the next morning. They were actually early. Josh had left a very apologetic voice message on Thomas' phone, but Thomas didn't get it until the drive to the field that morning. Thomas barely spoke to the renegades, except to let them know that they would have a formal conversation on the following Monday morning, well before anyone else arrived at the field. He set the meeting for 6:30am, and didn't expect them to show up at such an early time. Thomas re-posted job openings for camp assistant coaches for the remainder of the camp dates and scheduled two of the back-ups to work the following week.

The park was empty, and Thomas sat in his car, wondering if Joseph would show up in this weather. He realized how little he really knew about this man. Did Joseph even own a car? He didn't have Joseph's phone number or address. Didn't know what Joseph did for a living. For all he knew, Joseph could be a homeless man who liked discussing philosophy with anyone who might listen. It occurred to Thomas that he was expecting – or at least hoping for – a great deal of guidance from a man he barely knew. A man who just seemed to pop up here and there around town, but had never crossed Thomas' path before. Surely this was crazy. Thomas was early, but as the appointed time approached with no sign of Joseph, Thomas felt slightly relieved. He had done his homework, but the exercise was both harder than he had anticipated and left more questions than it answered. He felt very humbled by the exercise. C.S. Lewis had plenty to say about Thomas' current dilemma, but much of what he said wasn't what Thomas wanted to hear. He

123

brought many questions for Joseph, but the doubts that crept through his mind on this gray Saturday morning left him with a desire to avoid the conversation. It would be easier to go back. In a way, he felt like the character of Eustace on his first visit to Narnia in *The Voyage of the Dawn Treader*. He doesn't want to believe what all of his senses are confirming. Eustace keeps trying to convince himself that this world, this Narnia, is simply not real.

Tiff rather enjoyed hearing about this homework assignment and had even helped out quite a bit. She had been texting Thomas her thoughts in barrages since hearing about Joseph's challenge. In a way, this experience was quite an awakening. Thomas had also kept his commitment to praying every single morning, only now, he was bringing this question to his prayer time: *"How do the writings of C.S. Lewis pertain to Thomas' current predicament?"*

The rain grew heavier and Thomas was about to head back home when a tapping on his window startled him. Joseph was soaking wet and looming over the car, but his smile was warm. Thomas opened the window just a crack and the big man gestured towards a gazebo about fifty yards away. Before Thomas could respond, his companion was walking towards the gazebo, so Thomas got out and dashed to catch up.

There they sat, in the middle of an empty park in the rain. The notes Thomas had made in preparation were on his phone, but he had also printed a copy, which he handed to Joseph. Joseph looked through the pages, deep in thought, and with water still dripping from his beard and hair onto his shoulders. Thomas heard him utter an occasional "Hmmmph!" once an enthusiastic "yes, Yes!" and what sounded like a concerned, "oh, I see."

When Joseph had finished reading, he simply sat back, held the notes in one hand, and gestured with the other for Thomas to explain, so Thomas did. He tried to explain his approach to the assignment, first looking through the thoughts he had pulled out of *The Chronicles of Narnia* as he had been re-reading them. Then he had bought several other books by C.S. Lewis and perused them. He also scoured the internet, looking for relevant quotes by Lewis. He found it much easier to explain his process and provide the resources than it was to simply and clearly say where his findings led him. The conclusion was something he hoped Joseph would provide, but his hope was that Joseph would shed light on a different solution than the one Thomas kept seeing.

Finally, Thomas said, "Where does it all lead? As with most things, there can, of course, be many interpretations. Many solutions."

"Is that so?" Joseph's eyes had that twinkle Thomas had seen in their first meeting. The way he said this short sentence made it sound like Thomas had just said something incredulous, something that was blatantly false.

"Certainly," Thomas continued, although when he said the word, he felt everything but certain. As Thomas hemmed and hawed through his half-hearted explanation, Joseph placed his chin in the palm of his massive right hand, reminiscent of Rodin's statue of *The Thinker*, and rubbed his face in thought. Thomas rambled a bit longer before he ran out of things to say. He was speaking in circles and he knew it. He looked at Joseph and wasn't sure if the man was thinking about how to respond or just waiting for the right moment.

Slowly, Joseph pulled his hand away from his chin and held both hands out, open but facing Thomas with the palms up. The tone of his deep voice was more reassuring than his words. "Why are you afraid?" Joseph looked at Thomas until Thomas looked away.

"Afraid?" Thomas asked in response. "What do you mean?" Although he asked for clarification, both men knew that he already had it. How did Joseph pinpoint the trouble? Was he truly afraid? The emotion certainly felt like fear, but it was masked as uncertainty coupled with a thought that he should know the path. The problem was really rather simple. When he thought he knew the path, it was so contrary to the path he had followed for most of his life that he tried to make this new, yet correct, direction feel wrong.

"Thomas, this is what I see. You've done some of the most important research of your life. But the conclusion is not what you wanted it to be. I would like to talk about your findings, but may I first share a story?"

Thomas nodded. Joseph's voice must have been made for the telling of tales and he soon had Thomas enchanted by the short tale.

"The first few years of Jack's life were a fairy tale. He and his elder brother spent many carefree afternoons playing in the fields around their home by the sea in Northern Ireland. On rainy days – much like this one, and so very common in the old country – they would make up stories and often explore the attic of the family home." Joseph went on to tell of some of the boys' fantastic adventures, but all this was to change dramatically and suddenly. "Jack's brother, Warnie, was several years older and was sent off to boarding school. This dimmed the fairy tale childhood slightly, but Jack was so very close to his mother that the impact wasn't as great as it might have been. Good books, too. Young Jack was surrounded by good books. He would lose himself in them for hours and days upon end. That is, until Jack's ninth year. Cancer took his mother's life and Jack's distraught father decided to send the boy off to join Warnie at the boarding school. It was as if everything that mattered to Jack were ripped away from him, never to be seen again. In describing the time, he said that all happiness and security disappeared from his life – sunk like the continent of Atlantis. He asked why, like any child would, but found no sufficient answer. The questioning crept into all corners of his life, including an ultimate '*Why?*' Why do we exist? What could he believe in now? His very faith that there was good in the world, that there was purpose, that life had meaning – this was all open for questioning. And why shouldn't it be? He struggled to find meaning in his suffering, a suffering that didn't subside after a few days or weeks.

"Many years later, he wrote that he was living '... *in a whirl of contradictions. I maintained that God did not exist. I was also very angry with God for not existing. I was equally angry with Him for creating a world.*'

"Jack was known to most of the world by a different name, the name which appeared on his birth certificate, but throughout his life he preferred to be called by Jack. On official documents, he was known as C. S. Lewis.

"Thomas, there are bigger questions. We all have them. Throughout history, mankind has searched for answers to many questions, but four have persisted throughout all cultures and all times: destiny, origin, meaning, morality."

Thomas absorbed the story Joseph had just shared. So much of the story rang true, especially the teenage Jack living a life of contradiction. Living in *a whirl of contradictions.* He thought about his sister's idea that the truth sounds sweet to the ear. Thomas wasn't ready to just make a leap. He had prided himself for years on his tenacity in questioning assumptions. What assumptions were mired within this story? But, as he reflected on the nature of Lewis, he understood that the author had also questioned assumptions. Hunted down the answers might be a better way to describe it. He sought. It was different. Lewis sought and followed the quest for truth to its conclusion. In the realm of faith, Thomas had questioned, but questioning had been the chief aim, not finding answers.

Joseph had stopped speaking and was looking off at the river. A very light mist still hung in the air, but the rain had essentially stopped. Joseph stood up and took a few steps out from the shelter of the gazebo. Thomas stood up and ventured out into the wet grass.

Joseph continued. "Faith in a higher power, operates something like a deep and lasting friendship. When we have a friend that we trust, one that we can count on no matter what, do we have definitive proof that they will never betray us? We may certainly have sufficient evidence, past examples where they kept up their support. But we come to a point where we go on and trust. Faith works much like that. Do we all build deep friendships in the same amount of time? With the same number of fulfilled promises before freely giving the other person our trust? Of course, the answer is No. Seek. Ask questions – yes – but then seek answers. Thomas, there is such a word as truth. Our modern world seems to believe that the only wisdom humanity has ever displayed is within those currently alive. Therefore, the only history worthy of study is that which is not yet history. Countless great thinkers have pondered these facts. Socrates talked about and sought an '*Unknown God.*'

"What gets in the way? We do. For C.S. Lewis, or Jack as we now know him, there was the problem of pain. I think, at the end of the search, we all consider several choices. Among those choices two we have in common are these:

"First, either God does or does not exist. That question requires a yes or no answer. Many in the modern world want the answer to be a spectrum, but the question doesn't allow it. We can choose not to answer – or even to ask – the question, but if we do ask the question, it demands an answer.

"Second, what is the nature of God. This is a question that mankind continually struggles with. Perhaps we can look at this question in a binary fashion, as well. The question could be changed to this: Either God made man in His image or man attempts to make God in his. Put another way, either God is God, or we try to be God. We decide what rules we like and do not like. Either God creates purpose which we interpret and try to live, or we attempt to make our own purpose. Young Jack was certainly not alone in being challenged by this one. He wanted God's nature to not allow pain or suffering. His mother's untimely (according to whom?) death, World Wars, evil in general. Why should these things happen if God were what Jack wanted him to be?"

Both men had stopped walking and breathed in the damp fresh air. Thomas let the ideas mix around in his mind and soul. Several ideas blended with those already forming. Some provided roots where there had been none.

"What you're saying, it makes too much sense. But… Joseph, can I ask you a question? It may seem a little off the topic."

"Go ahead."

Thomas would normally have been more careful with the wording, but he didn't mind seeming unsure with Joseph. "I used to have so much more certainty, so much more clarity. I rarely doubted. But lately, I've been questioning myself more than I ever have. I told Clara – the mother of one of my campers – that I was lost and found. More lost than ever, but somehow feeling like I was not lost. It doesn't make sense."

"Hmmm. Interesting, but not surprising." Joseph chuckled. "From your notes, it appears that you've read all of *The Chronicles of Narnia*. Is that correct?"

"Not quite all of them. We have two books left – well, one and about a half. We're in the middle of The Silver Chair and then we'll read The Last Battle. But, I've taken quotes from all of them, some from the internet. And I've been re-reading those we've finished. Oh, by we, I mean my nephew, Ryan. We're reading them together!" Thomas energetically explained. A bit of pride swelled up within him as he spoke.

Joseph looked very pleased, the way Thomas' grandfather had often looked many years ago when he had taught Thomas something like fishing, or flipping a pancake. "Thomas, do you recall Eustace turning into a dragon on his first visit to Narnia?

"That would be hard to forget!"

"Of course. How was he able to change back to a boy?" Joseph's eyes narrowed as he watched Thomas thinking.

"Well, he pulled the scales off himself, didn't he?"

Joseph nodded with a crooked and all-knowing smile. "Yes, and no." He paused to let Thomas recall the fairy tale.

"That's right, he *tried* to pull the scales and dragon skin off of himself, but it didn't work. He tried it several times, peeling layer after layer of dragon skin off, but it was of no use. Eustace remained a dragon. That is, until Aslan tore – and very painfully, now that I think of it – the deepest layer of dragon skin off Eustace." Thomas smiled slightly and looked at the sun breaking through the clouds. In a faraway voice, he said, half to himself, "The undoing must be done." Thomas would go back and re-read this section of that book later. How did he miss this?

Renegade Coaches

Joseph broke the trance Thomas seemed to be in. "You told me much about your troubles. Can we take a new look at them? Tell me about the assistant coaches, the ones you referred to as the renegades."

Thomas filled in some more details on the way Ben had been strong-willed, resistant to any guidance, and filled with an acidic attitude that Thomas preferred the rest of the staff and campers not acquire. He even told Joseph about incorporating the challenges of running the camp into his daily commitment to prayer. With most people, he might not have mentioned the daily prayer, but with Joseph he had no reservations about discussing this. He did have a slight doubt that Joseph might see his prayer attempts as rather simplistic, but Joseph showed no signs of judgement, only that same grandfatherly look of pride.

When he had told everything he could think of, Joseph asked, "What should you do?"

Thomas expected to be told, rather than asked, what he should do. Joseph had emphasized the word *should*.

"Joseph, that's one of the many areas where I've been struggling. The old Thomas – in Narnian terms, I guess before peeling off a few scales, very few scales, mind you – would simply get rid of the problem. I still think that's what should be done. But as I pray about it, I keep thinking that there's another way. I just don't really see it. Some people change, but most don't. That's been my experience." Thomas stopped speaking and thought about what he had just revealed. The *old Thomas*, indeed!

"Thomas, do you see this as a continuation of our conversation about Eustace, then?"

"I do."

"This coach... Ben... do you love him enough to help him?" The words were bold, challenging, and direct. Then Joseph spoke in a gentler tone. "I spent much of my life answering small questions without answering the big ones. Over many years and too many missteps to count, I slowly started to figure out what I believed and why. Two big questions, upon which most, if not all, answers to the smaller questions rest. One such realization: God is never referred to as a grandfather. He's always referred to as a father."

Thomas laughed to himself, knowing that just a few months ago he would not have had the patience for what would have seemed to him like a philosophical discussion about nothing relevant to the real world. But today, Thomas knew the concept Joseph was unfolding would be worthy of consideration. He laughed again, thinking to himself, *I might even let this song affect me!*

Joseph continued, "Your nephew, did you say his name is Ryan?" Thomas nodded. "It seems your role with him is closer to that of a father than grandfather, or even uncle. Would you agree?" Another nod. "A good father loves his children, but doesn't let them off easy. A good father loves his children enough to be intensely interested in who they become. He cares enough to go through the pain of the journey with them. May I ask again; do you love Ben enough to help him?"

Thomas closed his eyes. He didn't want to look at Joseph. The answer was clear and burning. It made sense. He said it softly, apologetically. "No. No, I don't." He didn't look at Joseph when he said these words. The harsh, brutal admission stung. His mouth felt like it was swelling up, the way it would if his tongue were stung by a wasp. Joseph did not respond. There was no need. How often do we fill silence with unnecessary words when the silence, itself, was exactly what was needed?

They started to walk again and, when the conversation resumed, Thomas changed the subject to clouds, weather, and some traveling he hoped to do later in the summer. By the time they made their way back to Thomas's car, the warm sun caused a steam to rise from the wet pavement. They had agreed to meet at the same place on the following Saturday morning.

Revisiting Eustace the Dragon

Although many said Eustace was a different boy after the dragon incident, it would be more accurate to say that 'he began to be a different boy... The cure had begun.'

Thomas sat in Tiff's backyard, awestruck by what he had missed in his previous reading of *The Voyage of the Dawn Treader*. The big questions, what do I believe and why? Thomas kept coming back to this thought. Only a few hours after his morning with Joseph, he had received yet another email about a start-up that needed his expertise. His old life was calling. How great would it be to be rid of these troubles, these headaches, of dealing with college kids! It would be nice to be making decent money again, too, he thought.

What *should* he do was a very different question that what did he want to do or what did he feel like doing. This God as a father, not a grandfather paradigm rattled Thomas. In the grandfather role, God might let Thomas off the hook, just sticking with the "what do you want to do today" question. That one was easy to answer. I want to go back to making money, building a business, and not dealing with people that challenge me so much. For most of the people Thomas knew, entrepreneurship was a hard path, but for Thomas, it was the easier path. He got to call the shots. He always came up with good marketing strategies, so his businesses never really had to deal with customers if he decided they were too much trouble. They could replace the customer easily enough. What would a father – what would *The Perfect Father* – say he should do? Allowing his thoughts to go down this path was painful. He dropped to his knees in Tiff's backyard. It was dark, and Ryan was already asleep. With closed eyes, he felt like all the layers of skin and scales were being ripped from his body. It hurt. His heart hurt. His mind hurt. His body hurt.

A Day of Rest?

Small habits can have such a dramatic effect on our lives. Sunday had been merely another day for Thomas for so long. Over the last several weeks, however, he had made a commitment to doubling his prayer time on Sundays. Attending a church service had crossed his mind, but it hadn't happened... yet. Make Sunday a day of rest. He remembered this mantra from his childhood, but for years now it had been a great day to get things done – a buffer day to get caught up or even to get ahead. Work while others are sleeping.

He found some mantras of *Old Thomas* to be humorous now. It wasn't that they were bad concepts. He laughed for two reasons. First, the power of the mantras on his life made him realize that he had songs and philosophies that guided him long before meeting Joseph. Second, he recognized the theme in the mantras. The theme of the big questions, the mantra themes – and, naturally his resulting actions and habits – aligned themselves rather perfectly with his old unwritten mission. One word: *Success*. But what exactly did that word mean? He thought back to an interview he had seen on television just before the first phone call from the college that kicked off his career change. A very successful (there's the word success again, but in what way?) man was being asked his opinion on one of the hot topics of that month's news cycle. As the man responded, he brought up other opinions several times. What caught Thomas' attention and stuck was the way the man referred to these other sources. Each time, in various ways, the man described those who supported his opinion as "successful", "very successful", "runs a great business", while he pronounced those who disagreed as failures, disappointments, or generally unsuccessful. If the man expanded on his analysis of these individuals, most of the assessment hinged on financial and popularity measurements. Success, indeed.

On this particular Sunday, Thomas was pursuing success as a brother and uncle. He turned off the road and onto a long drive that meandered through a dense forest. Ryan called out from the back seat, "Whoa! Is this the adventure? Are we here?"

"We are here – but are you ready?" Thomas could anticipate his nephew's response.

"Oh yeah! But are you ready?" Ryan had echoed Thomas' words in this way so many times before.

Within minutes, they had backpacks on and were headed up a narrow winding trail. It had been a long time since Thomas last visited this spot. The sign said the hike was about four miles before they would arrive at the small lake. Was it really four miles? Thomas had a feeling that he might be carrying Ryan for a substantial distance. Tiff was wearing her backpack, too. She walked briskly and quietly, several yards ahead of the boys, and was lost in her thoughts. Shortly after setting out, Thomas and Ryan made several excursions off the trail to check out a tree that was perfect for climbing or a rock arrangement that must be the home to some sort of animal. Before they realized it, Tiff was out of sight.

There was nothing to worry about, Thomas thought to himself. Tiff had been here plenty of times before. As soon as this thought crossed his mind, he became suddenly aware of the reason Tiff was walking silently and briskly ahead. Why had he been so naïve? He should have remembered this earlier.

Tiff's last visit to the lake was with Paul, just days before he died. Thomas knew this, but it had somehow slipped his mind. How careless. Now, thinking back, he remembered the uneasy way Tiff had agreed to make the trip. How had he been so clueless?

A deep sadness began to permeate Thomas, but, simultaneously, a bitter anger bubbled up. Sure, he and Ryan were closer than ever, but he knew that he couldn't replace the little guy's dad. It just wasn't fair. This little boy would go to bed every single night for the rest of his life without being able to say goodnight to his dad.

He would never get to look into the stands at a baseball game – or any other sporting event – and see his dad smiling his approval. No dad at graduation or to help with homework, or to try to explain girls. No dad to teach him how to shave, or how to polish his shoes, thread a fishing hook, parallel park, change the oil. No dad. Thomas was fighting back tears and walking fast. A little too fast.

"Uncle Tommy! Wait for me!" Ryan was running on the path to catch up.

"Oh, sorry buddy." Thomas said it softly and put one hand up to his face to rub his eyes. He stopped and looked up at the trees. Nature had always been the place that he felt closest to his Creator, even if he wasn't so sure what that creator might be like. But now, as he took in a deep breath of the unspoiled and oxygen-rich forest air, his anger didn't subside. For the first time, he linked the emotion of anger with his friend Joseph. What would Joseph have to say about this – about his little innocent nephew having to grow up without a dad? Joseph, where's this God as a father when this happens? Thomas wanted an answer and he didn't expect that Joseph would have a suitable response. He would ask on their next meeting. He wasn't sure he'd be able to breach this topic without an air of condescension, but he would have the week to work on it.

Ryan caught up and reached out for his uncle's hand. Thomas tilted his head up towards the small patches of sky poking through the canopy of the treetops and closed his eyes for just a moment. Where are you in this, God? He wanted to be angry with God, too. And he was. He clenched his teeth, and tried to shake off the intense emotions. Today was a time to be with his nephew, his sister's baby boy. Today was a day of rest. Thomas decided that he would enjoy the hike and keep his emotions shut down. That is precisely what he tried to do.

The lake was as peaceful and pristine as a postcard. Tiff was sitting on a large rock, near the bank, and her head was tilted to one side.

Ryan ran to her, loudly calling out, "Mommy! Mommy!" He practically launched himself into her lap and said, "Wow, you were fast! But it wasn't a race, so you didn't win." Tiff laughed softly and hugged her little boy ever so close.

Thomas walked over to them and wasn't sure what expression he would see on his sister's face. What he did see came as quite a surprise. Peace. Joy. Those two words were the clearest way to describe what was written across her face. While anger and sadness had bombarded him, his sister sat by the lake full of peace and joy. He smiled, even though he didn't understand.

The three of them were silent, as they soaked in the peaceful lake with a clear reflection of the stunning blue sky and just a few small puffy clouds. *Day of rest. Day of rest.* Thomas was repeating the words silently to himself, in a way trying to remind himself of the purpose of this day and partly trying to re-convince himself that it was of some value. Why was there this constant nagging need to fill every minute with productive activity? What did it mean to be productive, anyway? His worldview had been rocked.

As he stood by the lake, Thomas' anger at God for his brother-in-law's death made several attempts to return. Its approach was much like that of a sly fox. He consciously resisted thinking about it. Today was not the day. Now was not the time. But the thoughts kept returning and their approach was clever. He'd notice a tree perched precariously along the bank of the lake because the water had eroded the soil around one side of its roots. Surely the erosion would eventually cause the tree to crash down into the lake. Thomas thought about death, dying, and unfair circumstances. Did the tree have any way to avoid these circumstances that would eventually kill it? Of course not. Thomas had to stop himself from going further down this path. The temptation to continue this thought process returned many times that afternoon. He would look over at Ryan and a thought about the little guy needing help on his homework would pop into his head. Thomas would fight it back.

Then he'd see Tiff walking and that sly fox of temptation would give him a glimpse Tiff eating dinner alone for years and years to come and working a second job just to get by. Time after time he fought off the temptations to become angry. Today was a day of rest, he said to himself, only it felt more like a day of guilt, resentment, and anger. No! Thomas almost had to shout inside his own head. Stop! Enough! Today, I will be with my sister and nephew. They had hiked halfway back to the parking lot before Thomas finally won the battle in his head. How did he win? He wasn't sure and didn't want to think about it for fear of the bitterness creeping back into his thoughts.

That last stretch of the hike back to the car was a most beautiful experience. Ryan was the trail guide, the leader of the expedition, and his enthusiasm for pointing out things they passed was contagious. Tiff made her role in the game come alive. One minute she would be enthralled by moss growing on a rotting tree or a slimy crawling creature; the next minute she was a frightened traveler, quivering as she explained to Ryan the Guide about a sound she had heard in the distance. She deserved an award for her acting performance. Was a herd of beasts hunting them? Would Ryan be able to protect them from imminent danger? Thomas joined the game, as well, tossing a rock into the woods ahead of them and then stopping suddenly to ask what the sound could have been. Then the three sang a few songs together. Ryan sang loudly and, as they approached the car, he started singing one of his favorites, This Land is Your Land. Thomas had to smile. The day didn't go the way he had planned and the battle for his mind was intense, but all in all, it had been a great day. This day of rest thing deserved a place in life's routine.

On the ride home, Ryan said something that would keep Thomas' attention for the rest of the week.

Tiff kept asking her little boy questions so that he could recount their entire adventure. It was something she did quite often, and

Thomas appreciated her patience and persistence with Ryan. Thomas wasn't really involved in the conversation but was listening to the back and forth between mother and son. He loved the way Tiff stayed right with Ryan, modifying her energy, pace, and level of curiosity to keep up an incredible dance of communication – words, pauses, questions, facial expressions.

Then Tiff asked a question that opened the door. "Ryan, what was your favorite thing to imagine on our hike?"

"The Black Knight," came his response, almost instantly.

"The Black Knight! What? Where?" Tiff responded without missing a beat and with such an admirable sincere curiosity. *If only every mother would enter her child's world like this more often,* thought Thomas.

"By the bridge." Ryan expected his mother to remember the bridge, but she waited for him to clarify. "Mom, remember that gigantic tree going across the stream? It was pretty high up and I – I mean the guide – had to be the brave one to cross it first?"

"Oh yes, that bridge! The stream was so far below us. There's no way we would've made it without such an amazing guide."

Thomas shuddered in a silent laughter at this interchange.

"I imagined it was the bridge that Eustace and Pole – oh, and Puddleglum – crossed when they saw the Black Knight and the green lady... what was she called?" Then his voice got louder. "Uncle Tommy, what was she called?"

No response.

"Uncle Tommy!" He was a bit loud, but just from excitement. "What was the green lady called? Remember? The green lady with the Black Knight? On the bridge."

Thomas recalled the scene very well. He had just re-read it a few days ago and shook his head at the coincidence of Ryan bringing this up. That scene was hard to forget.

"Wasn't she the *Lady of the Green Kirtle*?" Thomas pronounced.

"Yeah! Yeah! That's her name. What a weird name, right Mommy? Lady of the Green Kirtle. I don't even know what a green kirtle is. What is it?"

"Maybe Uncle Tommy can help explain. Uncle Tommy?" Tiff's tone said that she was teasing her brother. She didn't know and wasn't sure the all-knowing Thomas would, either.

"I believe that a kirtle is a type of dress or cloak. What does our guide think? Would a green dress or cloak fit with the story?"

"Yeah, it's a cloak." Ryan appeared satisfied for having filled in a missing piece to the story. "Anyway, that big tree was like the bridge they crossed and she – the lady – was on the other side with the Black Knight. And she tricked them."

"No, she didn't!" exclaimed Tiff.

"Yup. She told them all kind of things that they wanted to hear to get them to forget about their mission."

"What? Was she one of the bad guys?" Tiff asked.

"Of course, Mommy. She's an evil witch." Ryan's eyes were wide with disbelief that his mother didn't know this. Tiff shook her head in astonishment and a look of fear flashed across her face. Ryan was pleased to see that he had helped her to understand.

Tiff was cherishing this experience with her little boy. So often it was easy to get caught up in the routine and forget to just be with him, connect with him, seize the day with him. She asked, "Was the bridge dangerous – or scary – to the travelers?" She didn't remember hearing anything about the bridge from either Thomas or Ryan before this.

"Not the bridge, Mommy. The Lady and the Knight. They were a little scary, but not to me. Mostly to Puddleglum. I think he was scared of them."

"Oh, I see. What was scary about them?" Tiff was laughing inside at the way a mother so often gets to put a story together backwards, sideways, or in some random order from the pieces she catches in between everything else it takes to try to keep family life clicking along.

Ryan must have thought about this a bit. "Well... Eustace and Pole liked the Lady and Knight. But not Puddleglum. He didn't. He didn't trust them. The other two were so excited about warm beds, and taking a bath – I don't know why taking a bath is so exciting – they just wanted to get to the place the Lady talked about. Puddleglum wasn't so sure that it was a good idea. She tricked them, right Uncle Tommy?"

"Yes, she did." Thomas was surprised that the boy remembered this section of the book so clearly. During this interchange, he caught a glimpse of the impact a story can have on a child's life. Ryan must have felt like he was part of the journey with the three travelers. Ryan's lesson from the story was just beginning.

"So, she tricked them?" Tiff asked Ryan.

"Yeah. And it was really easy. I think they wanted to be tricked. She just told them about warm beds and baths and food. They almost forgot about everything else." Ryan stopped speaking and looked out the window at the passing scenery.

The BMW ate up these winding roads and Thomas was enjoying the twists and turns when he felt Ryan tapping him on the shoulder. Apparently, Ryan had once again called his uncle's name a few times while Thomas was off in his own world, but the tapping brought him back.

"Uncle Tommy, it's kind of the same thing, isn't it?"

"What, Ryan? What's kind of the same thing?" Thomas wasn't sure if he had missed the first part of the question.

"Well, at camp, Willie tells us all the time that if we want to be good, it won't be easy. How does he say it? Good isn't easy? No. It's something like that. Trade good and easy? Can you call Willie and ask him?"

Thomas knew the phrase that Ryan was looking for. It was a phrase that one of his own coaches had used years ago. "Don't trade good for easy."

"Yeah! Don't trade good for easy! Willie says that when we sometimes don't want to do the same drill over and over, or when we get distracted and are goofing off. That's what Puddleglum was trying to get them not to do. They wanted the trip to be easier and when the Lady promised them all that stuff – the warm beds and yummy food – they forgot all about Aslan's mission."

Wow! Thomas stared at the road ahead with his mouth hanging half-opened. The same exact thing had happened to him on this commitment to daily prayer time. Distractions. Easy got in the way of good. A warm bed, a long hot breakfast, all types of nice distractions side-tracked him from this mission that mattered so deeply.

The Monday Morning Meeting

Thomas arrived significantly early for the "meeting" on Monday morning. He was shocked to see Ben and Josh already at the field, sitting on the dugout bench. Thomas shut the car off and sat in it quietly for a few moments. The plan he had worked on for this meeting seemed so clear and simple over the last few days and even earlier that morning, when he had taken it to his prayer time. But now he could feel his blood pressure rising and his resentment growing. It was, after all, justified. What these two arrogant college kids had done to his camp was unacceptable. Thomas was mad and had every right to be. Before he opened the car door, the challenge Joseph had issued came back to him. "Do you love him enough to help him?" What did that even mean? As his frustration and bitterness towards these two kids increased, Thomas wanted to ignore the words of guidance. But he couldn't. Instead, he closed his eyes and recalled how he had prayed about this over the last several days and brought that question into his prayer. A peace flooded his mind. He likened the word *love* with *care*. Do I care about these boys? Do I care about their future? Do I care that they become more responsible, that they learn some of life's most important lessons? Do I care about the positive – or negative – influence they can have on others, not just in the camp, but in their lives? Do I care the way a father would care? This last question stopped him in his tracks. His eyes opened wide and his jaw was set. How? How does Joseph understand this so well? How did he, Thomas, not see it before? Part of his job as the camp director, as the coach, as Uncle Tommy, was to care the way a father cares. Thomas opened the door. He was as ready for this conversation now as he ever would be.

Ben and Josh looked up as Thomas approached.

144

Don't Trade Good for Easy

The following Saturday was a hot one. There was no sign of rain on this morning. Although he arrived early, Thomas found Joseph already sitting at their bench.

"Let us walk together, my friend." The old man's voice always had a warmth to it. Thomas struggled to describe it until that morning. Joseph stood up and they walked along the river together for several minutes without speaking. Thomas had a good week at camp. He also had a list of questions for his friend. As they walked, he thought about the best place to start, but Joseph beat him to it.

Joseph said the words slowly and deliberately, but with joy, "I didn't go to religion to make me happy. I always knew a bottle of Port would do that. If you want a religion to make you feel really comfortable, I certainly don't recommend Christianity." After a deep hearty laugh, he continued. "Jack said that. Our dear friend, C.S. Lewis. I would tend to agree. What say ye, Thomas?"

Thomas had grown to expect, to welcome, to appreciate – the challenges posed by his friend. "Comfortable. It's a lot like easy. My nephew – well, really one of my coaches – reminded me of an old lesson. 'Don't trade good for easy.' But your quote... I mean Jack's quote... don't most people look for a belief system that makes them feel comfortable, perhaps even one that's easy?"

Joseph's deep laugh caught Thomas off guard. "Whoa! Ah-hah! Right into the deep end we go, yes?" Joseph's strong arm slapped Thomas on the back. "That topic, Thomas, could keep us quite busy for years."

Thomas had hoped for a simple answer, but realized that this truly was a topic that begged for much discussion. "Well, I suppose we can start with where I was – or am." Joseph's expression gave Thomas the approval to continue. "If I were to be honest, I think I've been looking for a faith that fits what I want, a faith that's easy, comfortable."

"Yes. And how has that worked out? What have you found?" The way Joseph said these words reflected the man's wisdom.

"No. I mean, I haven't found much. It hasn't worked out very well. But shouldn't it be comfortable?" Thomas asked Joseph, but was really asking himself. The truth was, he had often just dismissed any real and personal search for a strong faith by hiding behind questions like these and untested assumptions that faith should be simple, or easy, or convenient, or tailored to your own experience, or what works for the individual.

Joseph stopped walking and looked out over the river. "Tell me, Thomas, can you walk across the river? Right now, if you walked across this river, would you sink, or would you walk upon the water's surface?"

"Sink, of course."

"Yes. I do believe that you would."

Thomas waited for Joseph to explain. The large man allowed Thomas' curiosity to build before continuing.

"The expression 'true for you' is one of mankind's greatest fallacies in logic. You see, Thomas, we both know that you would either sink or walk upon the water. One of these options is true. The same holds for the existence of God, as we discussed in our last meeting. Thomas, may I ask you another question?"

"You just did, my friend." The two laughed at this comment and then Thomas said, "If I were to say no, would that stop you from asking?"

"It would not." Joseph turned to face his friend and looked into his eyes before asking, "Is everything meant to be understood? Is that the point of life?"

"No, I certainly don't believe understanding everything is *the* point of life. But, that doesn't mean I – I mean people – just have to accept everything without understanding." Thomas resented the tone that accompanied his answer.

"Thomas, let's go back to walking across the water. Boats are able to float and, with the appropriate speed, glide across the surface of the water. Do all people understand the physics behind what makes a boat float or glide?"

"Not all."

"Some people do, while some do not. Does one need to understand the physics in order to get into a boat and trust that it will carry them?"

"No."

"In some ways, faith operates similarly. You can certainly get answers to many of your questions. But there may be some that you and I never completely understand. Do we like it that way? Do we think it *should* operate that way? Perhaps not. Again, we go back to that idea: Either we are made in God's image, or we try to make God in our own. Throughout history, mankind has battled between accepting God's ways and re-evaluating God's ways. We have a tendency to become proud. And, as Lewis so powerfully reminded us, '*As long as you are proud you cannot know God. A proud man is always looking down on things and people; and, of course, as long as you are looking down you cannot see something that is above you.*'"

"Hmmm," was Thomas' response. But the simple idea that God didn't have to make things perfectly comfortable didn't seem to answer the real challenge Thomas had been struggling with. He decided that now was the time to dive in. His words came out in a challenging and surprisingly sarcastic tone. "Sure. That all makes sense, but help me with this one: why is the world full of so much bad, so many disasters, so many people in pain?" He stopped for a few seconds, realizing the hypocrisy of his statements. "Yeah, I get that I'm making God in my image, but what kind of all-powerful being lets people go through so much suffering? It's just not fair." Thomas' words were soaked with the bitter sorrow he had fought so hard to hold back during the hike on the previous Sunday.

Joseph didn't respond straight away. He could tell that this was one of the big issues. Instead, he took a deep breath and nodded slowly, signaling that he understood were Thomas was coming from.

When he finally spoke, his voice was soothing. "Thomas, my dear friend Thomas, I don't believe I've ever come across someone with a deep faith who didn't wrestle with questions from time to time. In the bible, there is a story of Jacob wrestling with God and then God gives him a new name, Israel, which means to wrestle with God. Would you agree that some ideas are truly worth wrestling with?"

"Wow. 'Israel' means wrestle with God? I didn't know that." Thomas wondered how this man knew so much. "Yes. The answer is yes. Some ideas are worth wrestling with."

Joseph started walking again and shared a story. "Thomas, I'm sure you are familiar with the story of David and Goliath?"

"Of course."

"We each have our own Goliaths, Thomas. In our spiritual journey, too often we choose not to face those Goliaths. They could be the concepts we don't understand, or areas where we disagree with our faith. Therein lies a great choice. Will we study the topic, learn enough to understand it, or just use it as an excuse to stay with the easy and comfortable choice?"

"Lean into the discomfort." Thomas said quietly. "In baseball, so many hitters do well until they get to that next level of pitching. And suddenly, they find they can't hit a curve, or a cut fastball that starts on the corner of the plate before breaking out of the strike zone. It's the same thing. The game humbles them before they look for answers. If they don't lean in, get to know that pitch, 'wrestle with the curve or cut fastball', they can hang up their hat, bat and glove. So many do. Joseph, they don't face their Goliath." Even though it was still very early in the morning, the sun was already hot, and Thomas had to wipe beads of sweat from his face. It was easier to talk about baseball or stories from the past, but Thomas knew this conversation had extremely important personal implications. He chose not to avoid them. "Joseph, what do you recommend? I mean for me, not for fixing the world."

"Agreed, Thomas, let us fix you before moving on to the rest of the world." The two shared a good laugh. The laughter was much needed, as this topic was tough. Joseph's advice was timed and worded perfectly. "Dig in. Thomas, dig in to the topic that is troubling you. Study it. Research it. Wrestle with it. Look for giants who have wrestled with this same topic and see if you can stand upon their shoulders. Perhaps a good source to start with would be a book on this topic by our very own C.S. Lewis. He wrote of his wrestling and called it *The Problem of Pain*."

"Yes. Thank you, Joseph."

Their time together was almost up, but Joseph could tell that Thomas was hurting. The walk had taken them back to that old park bench. Joseph sat down slowly, but Thomas remained standing, knowing that it was time to get going, but not wanting his time with this wise man, his friend, to end. Joseph looked up at Thomas and blocked the sun from his eyes with one hand. "Do you have time for a very short story before you get on your way?"

"One of your stories, Joseph? Most certainly!" Thomas took a few steps to the side so Joseph wouldn't have to keep looking towards the sun. He was thrilled to hear just one more crumb of wisdom and was sure that his anticipation was written across his face.

"A large bear was caught in a hunter's trap, deep in the woods. When the hunter approached, the bear was in pain and immediately saw the hunter as a threat. The hunter, however, had not set the trap for the bear and had no intentions of harming the magnificent and powerful creature. As the hunter approached, the bear growled fiercely, expecting the hunter to be his enemy. The hunter knew he would stand no chance at setting the bear free unless the bear cooperated and, since the bear showed no signs of cooperating, the hunter took out a tranquilizer gun and shot the bear. One tranquilizer dart wasn't enough, so he shot the bear with a second dart. The second dart had the intended effect, and soon the bear was quite groggy and barely – pardon the pun – moving. As the hunter approached, the bear was still conscious, and made a slight growl at him. The hunter wrestled with the trap and was finally able to free the bear's hind paw. Now, a few questions about the story. Who has more knowledge, more understanding, the bear or the hunter?"

"The hunter, naturally."

"Right. Did the bear understand that the hunter wanted what was best for the bear?"

"No."

"When the hunter pointed his tranquilizer at the bear and fired, what was the bear thinking?"

"I'm sure when he felt the pain, he was confirming his expectation that the hunter was going to harm, or even kill, him."

"Then the hunter fired a second shot. What does the bear think now?"

"More of the same."

"When the hunter is pulling on and bending the bear's leg to get it out of the trap, the bear is still conscious. It probably still hurts. What's he thinking then?"

"The hunter is the enemy."

"Yes! Sure, the hunter's ways and thoughts are higher than the bear's, but God's ways and thoughts are infinitely higher than ours. He sees things from a different time-table, in light of eternity. Do you think God might allow us to experience pain and suffering that will mold and shape us, that will set us free?"

By this point, Thomas had both hands covering his face. He rubbed his eyes and brought his hands to a folded and prayerful position in front of his chin.

Joseph stood up to embrace his friend. They said their goodbyes, planned to meet on the following Saturday, and parted company.

A Little Sisterly Guidance

Thomas stopped at a bookstore later that morning and bought a copy of Lewis' book, *The Problem of Pain*. He read half of the short book before lunch time and tossed it on the passenger seat of his car. He had promised Ryan they could go to the park for some baseball later that afternoon. As the sun beat down, the day grew ever hotter, so Thomas was relieved when he read Tiff's text message. Tiff wrote, "The boys want to go swimming for a few hours. Can baseball wait till later this evening?"

Thomas was quick to reply, "Sure." And then "BoyS?" He thought it could be an autocorrect typo, but Tiff didn't frequently refer to her son as 'boy'.

"Oh, Joey is hanging out with us for the afternoon. Can he play baseball with you?"

Another "Sure."

Then the next round of Tiff's secret plan swung into action. "Almost forgot... Clara's painting some rooms. Needs help moving some furniture. Today. The sooner the better. I offered your assistance. What are sisters for? Thanks!"

Almost forgot? Thomas had planned to get some things done around his own house that weekend. But his sister *almost forgot* that she had volunteered his services and *the sooner the better*. What a sister! But he had to admit that helping Clara out was an appealing way to spend his afternoon. Within minutes, he was staring into his closet and trying to decide what to wear for moving furniture and painting. *Ridiculous*, he thought to himself. I don't worry about what I'm wearing. Just throw on old shorts and a work-around-the-house t-shirt. He tried that, but found himself changing twice before heading out the door, shaking his head at his unprecedented wardrobe indecision.

Clara didn't answer the door. Thomas knocked a few more times, but could hear loud music pouring through the open windows. He knocked louder and called her name. Still no response, so he turned the handle. The door opened, and Thomas walked in, calling our "Hello! Helloooooo!" as he walked through the house towards the source of the music. Clara startled him as she appeared in the hallway just in front of him. In her hands was a stack of small cards with various paint color schemes.

"Do you know anything about paint?" Clara didn't skip a beat, but kept walking right past Thomas and towards the front door.

"A little. I've done my share of painting. I probably know more about what not to do and what paints and brushes not to buy. How to speckle paint the floor while painting the walls and ceiling is something I've mastered! Would that help?"

She laughed as Thomas went on to describe one of his messiest painting experiences. Clara pointed both of her index fingers up at the ceiling, down at her floor, then directly at Thomas, and finally through the window and towards Thomas' car. "Let's go. That's exactly the kind of help I need."

"Where are we going?"

"To pick out paint, brushes, rollers, everything. Would you be so gracious as to assist me, kind sir?" Clara adopted her best British accent.

Thomas went along. "My lady, I could think of no more exciting way to spend the afternoon. Shall I escort you there in my coach?"

Thomas continued the charade of exaggerated chivalry, opening his car's passenger door as Clara quite properly got in and sat down. Clara rather formally picked up the book from her seat as her eyes scanned the author and title. She uttered a polite and all-knowing "Hmmm. Rather curious title." She handed the book to her chauffeur. "Are you rather enjoying the book?" she inquired.

"No. To be fair, I'm not exactly enjoying it so far."

"Really, is that so? It's not a good book, then? Why, may I be so bold to ask, would a busy gentleman such as yourself continue reading a book that's not very good?" Clara teased, continuing her wonderful British accent.

Thomas let out a little laugh. "Ha hah! Very funny. It is a very good book, but that's not what you asked, my lady. You asked if I'm enjoying it. And no, I am not. What I mean is that it's not an easy read. It shakes you up. It rings true."

"Oh, I see. Is the coach getting some coaching?"

Thomas looked into her eyes and could see a wonderful and caring heart. "You, Clara, are quite funny. But then I'm rather certain that you already know that!"

"Funny indeed, sir. Is that your way of avoiding the question? Does it often work for you?" She smiled an all too knowing smile.

"Avoid a question? Me? *Never!*" Thomas realized after the words left his mouth that his tone and volume were just a bit edgy. He thought he might have sounded very much like Sir Winston Churchill with that last "Never!"

Thomas realized that he had correlated the increased volume of his voice with a more aggressive driving stance and was now heading into a tight turn at a substantial speed. Taking hard turns was nothing new for him, but not all passengers were used to his driving style. By the time he processed all of this, it was too late to slow down, so he plowed through the turn. The tires and suspension of his performance convertible had no problem with this, but the passenger might be a different story. As the car exited the turn, Thomas eased off the gas pedal, loosened his grip on the steering wheel, and glanced over at Clara. She hadn't made a sound and looked like she might be holding her breath.

Clara was the first to speak. "Okay, then." She nodded her head slightly.

"Yeah, okay." The words came out softly and with a distant tone. Thomas wasn't exactly sure what her okay was referencing. Was it his driving move or his loud "*Never!*" response to her challenge of avoiding a question? He hoped it wasn't both and realized that neither had happened the way he would have wanted. Was he just some kind of a jerk? She must have been wondering this. Thomas wished he could take back just that last 60 seconds. Just one minute. Why is it so easy to mess things up in a minute? He didn't know what to say, so he just slowed the car to a more reasonable speed and continued towards the hardware store.

Clara had been holding her breath. Driving a car around a sharp turn like Thomas just had was not something she often did. She picked up the book once again, modifying, but not entirely changing, the topic. "What got you to read this – this, oh how did you put it… not really enjoyable, but challenging – book?"

Before Thomas could answer, Clara excitedly said, "C.S. Lewis! I love him. Isn't he – he must be the same C.S. Lewis that wrote *The Lion, the Witch and the Wardrobe*?"

"Yes, he is that very same person." Thomas took a deep breath and felt relieved. Clara read the back cover and began flipping through its pages. Either the book or Thomas' highlights and notes in the margins certainly had Clara's attention. She paused to read further on many pages and he could see that she was deep in thought.

By the time they arrived at the paint aisle, their cart held a collection of brushes, rollers, sandpaper, scrapers, spackling compound, and two new light switch covers. Clara was caught up in evaluating color options and excitedly shared options and her thoughts out loud.

"Oh, this combination! What do you think?" She held up yet another pair of paint color cards for Thomas to see. Thomas couldn't help but think about how different this was from his last paint purchase. White walls. White ceiling. That trip had been quick. Efficient. But he had to admit that he rather enjoyed Clara's enthusiasm. It took much longer than Thomas would have anticipated to settle on colors, but they did get out of the store with all the necessary supplies.

On the drive home, Clara asked to borrow the book, *The Problem of Pain*, when Thomas was finished with it. Thomas agreed, wondering if his notes in the margins might be too self-revealing. They worked together to tape off the trim areas and ceiling. Thomas would do the trim work while Clara used the roller.

"I loved that book – his other book, I mean." Clara said suddenly.

"Which book?"

"Narnia. The Lion, the Witch –"

"Yes, what a great story!" Thomas realized he had interrupted her and apologized. "Sorry for interrupting. You were about to say…"

She wasn't bothered by the interruption and continued. "What was the word? Oh, it was so long ago. I read the story when I was a little kid. The girl meets the fawn and – it was so funny – she tells him something about her world and he gets the word wrong. What was that word?" something she says but he misunderstands."

"Spare Oom." Thomas remembered. "Yes, Lucy meets Mr. Tumnus and tells him that she came from the wardrobe in the spare room. He thinks 'Spare Oom' is her country."

"Spare Oom! Yes, that's it. I loved that part. Mr. Tumnus, that's right. That was the Fawn's name." Clara's face lit up as Thomas imagined it must have when she first read the book as a child.

He loved to see this exuberance and asked question he hoped would keep her reminiscing. "What was it about the mixed-up words that you liked so much?"

"Oh, I don't really know. Maybe…" She crinkled her nose and looked off into space, searching her memory from many years ago. "I guess it was that when we don't understand something we make up our own version. Something like that. Our own version must sound so funny to someone who knows the real story, or what the real word is – what the real word means. I can remember changing a lot of other expressions after reading that. Maybe I was nine or ten?"

Thomas wanted Clara to continue and quietly asked, "What kind of expressions did you change? Do you remember any of them?"

She laughed out loud. "Thomas, it was crazy kid stuff. I changed so many words! It went on for days and days. I must have made my parents and teachers crazy. Some of them were good, but some were just ridiculous. It wasn't just the words. As I invented the words, I would create all kinds of scenarios to use these new words. I turned funny into Fu Knee, house into How's, carrot into Kah-rot…" Clara burst into laughter. "That's just it, some of the words took on a life of their own. I had definitions, sometimes even the origins of the word. Kah-rot was a type of rot that formed on vegetables that made them poisonous only if they were cooked. A scientist in the small African village of Kah had discovered this rot. Most people were unaware of the rot, so they would still try to get their children to eat cooked vegetables, but children's taste buds were able to detect the Kah-rot. My mother loved when I pushed my cooked carrots aside because they had Kah-rot. Needless to say, my game became quite popular with some of my friends for a short time."

The painting work didn't really feel like work at all. A few hours passed quickly, as the two traded stories from childhood, moments that each cherished, and experiences that had helped shape perspective. They laughed, sang a few songs, and even shed a few tears together. By late afternoon, the painting was nearly complete.

Clara looked over the work and then paused, locked eyes with Thomas, and asked, "Thomas, how things are going with the camp?" She held eye contact for several seconds before looking away. "I mean, Joey loves it. I'm not asking about him – or about how he's doing." She was searching for the right way to ask her question. "How are *you* doing with the camp?" She hoped her words didn't come across as a challenge or with a tone that assumed something wasn't going well.

"Good. Pretty good." He resurfaced. Even though they had talked about so many real things that afternoon, he reverted to his standard operating procedure. Don't discuss things that you aren't sure you are handling well, things that might not be working out the way they should. Should. There's that word again.

"What was that?" Clara moved slightly nearer to him. "Did you say *should?*"

He didn't realize that he had said the word aloud. Did he sound uncertain? Could he recover? Or was it time to put this on the table? He stammered, "Yeah, I did. Should. I don't know, I just think things should work out a certain way. And when they don't go the way they should, I..."

She interrupted. Her facial expression seemed to say that she absolutely had to interrupt, so Thomas stopped to let her. "Thomas, aren't there other Narnia books?"

"Yes. There are seven." He wasn't sure how or if this was related.

"Do the children go back to Narnia again?"

"Yes."

"How?"

"I'm not sure what you mean?"

"How do they return to Narnia? Is it always through the Wardrobe in Spare Ooom?"

"Oh. No. They – well, it's not even always the same children – but they do not use the War Drobe after that first adventure. They get to Narnia many different ways."

"Perfect!" She seemed extremely pleased with this answer.

"I guess." Thomas was thinking about the variety of methods used throughout the books. He didn't recall them all immediately. "There was a painting, a train station. Oh, and the rings! Clara, why did you say it was perfect?"

"It's perfect because of that word – your word – should!"

"Yeah, should." His mouth opened as he thought about this. "I imagine that the children thought that they should – yes, *should!* – be able to get back to Narnia the same way, and whenever they chose. Actually, Ryan has said this to me many, many times. He'll say, 'If I were Peter, I would go back in the wardrobe all the time.' But it doesn't work that way! You're good, Clara."

She nodded her head slightly, accepting the praise, then quickly turned and jogged out to his car, returning with that book in her hands. She was excitedly searching, flipping through the pages.

"There it is! She read one of his highlighted lines slowly and deliberately. *'God allows us to experience the low points of life in order to teach us lessons that we could learn in no other way.'* Thomas, it shouldn't be like that, should it?" She was smiling, teasing him, but he didn't mind this time. "If I'm honest – perhaps I shouldn't be?" She let out a quiet and innocent teasing laugh before continuing. "If I'm honest, I don't really want it to be that way. I don't want to experience the low points. I don't want the struggles. That's the point of his title, isn't it? *The Problem of Pain.* We don't want it, but we need it. It molds us, shapes us."

Thomas was nodding. He shared the story of the bear, hunter, and trap. As he finished the story, Clara was biting on her lower lip, her face awash with emotion.

"Thomas, I want to tell you about Joey's father." Her eyes were closed as she began. Thomas just listened as Clara explained that Joey's father had simply left. A lot happened leading up to his departure, but for over a year, she considered everything to be his fault. Something he said the day before he left had been etched into her memory. "No one can live up to your expectations. No one." Those words stayed with her. They bothered her. Slowly, she had allowed the truth of this statement to work its way into her heart. Did she have high expectations? Of course. Why shouldn't she? Over many sleepless nights, many days of torment, she started to realize the judgement that she often exuded. It was a judgement not only towards Joey's father, but towards her friends, other family members, herself, and even little Joey.

"Thomas, I needed to learn to love. It was one of the most painful experiences of my life, not one I would ever want to relive or wish on anyone. I was loneliness, bitterness, self-pitying. I was not a very good mom during that time. Not that I'm perfect now, don't get me wrong! But loving is not a word that would describe me during that time. Demanding? Sure. Prideful? You bet. And blaming everyone else for my circumstances."

She opened the book and read the words again, this time soaked with a wave of gratitude. *"God allows us to experience the low points of life in order to teach us lessons that we could learn in no other way."*

Thomas was stunned with what he had just heard. He couldn't imagine Clara being described as demanding, prideful, or blaming. He leaned forward with his elbows on his knees and his head in his folded hands.

"Thomas, can I hug you?"

"Sure," he replied softly.

And she did.

But How, Joseph, HOW?

"Joseph, how do you do it?" The two were sitting at their bench very early on a warm Saturday morning.

"Do what, Thomas?"

"Gather wisdom. Make wise decisions. Remember all these ideas, phrases. Have the right expression, idea, or story for the situation. Joseph, how do you do it?"

Joseph looked away modestly. "Would you mind if we come back to that question later? Please tell me about your progress. How is the camp going?"

Thomas filled Joseph in on the most recent interaction he had as coach with Ben, his most challenging assistant. The plan seemed good, but it didn't go the way he had hoped.

One particular interaction stuck out most. "Just. Follow. The program." Thomas had said each part of his instruction slowly and deliberately, using his right hand to motion up and down for effect. An ingenuine "Thank you," were his words as he had turned and walked away. The interaction had been incredibly cold and Thomas reflected on it many times throughout the week

Joseph listened intently, asking a few very pertinent questions. One that Thomas struggled to answer was, "What did the young man feel from you?"

Thomas tried to respond. "Well… What did he feel? I don't know." Joseph waited patiently so Thomas knew that he had to continue. "He probably felt berated. Beaten down. Not valued." He couldn't believe the words as they came out of his mouth.

Thomas repeated his earlier question. "How, Joseph, how do you do it? Really, just a few weeks ago, I was sure that I had to just get rid of my problem. Now I've been starting to think that the problem is actually my most important lesson. Only I'm not doing very well with it. Maybe I should have just gone with my first instinct and sent him packing."

"Hmmm," was Joseph's response. This great man was deep in thought. The sun was beginning to bring a steady warmth to the morning air. Thomas tilted his head back to feel the sun on his face. He wondered why he expected his friend, Joseph, to have the right answers. But this high expectation had been consistently met.

The old man started slowly, with a deep respect and care in his voice. "What if – Thomas – what... if... it is not about you?"

Under any other circumstances, Thomas would have resisted, perhaps even resented, a statement such as this. But he did not, and Joseph continued. *"No man knows how bad he is till he has tried very hard to be good.* Those words are not mine, but C.S. Lewis's. He also said, '*Everyone thinks forgiveness is a lovely idea until he has something to forgive.*'"

Oh, was this ever true. Thomas reflected for a moment on some of the painting conversation with Clara, and then on a few of his own attempts to be *good.*

Thomas' thoughts were interrupted as he felt Joseph's strong hand clasped on his shoulder. When he looked over at his friend, he saw a large, almost childish smile spread across the man's face. Joseph chuckled in a way that seemed appropriate for a shared inside joke. But Thomas didn't know the cause of the laughter. Joseph laughed again and, as he saw Thomas' face clearly showing confusion, the old man explained the reason for his laughter.

"Thomas, I'm laughing about your reading adventure with that nephew of yours, Ryan. Something quite funny happened aboard the *Dawn Treader.*"

Thomas tried to recall some of the funny scenarios from the book, still hoping to unwrap this inside joke of Joseph's.

Joseph continued, "Our friend Eustace – Eustace Clarence Scrubb – do you recall that he kept a journal throughout the adventure?"

"Yes, I do."

"Thomas, what was that journal used for back in England, before the adventure to Narnia?"

"Uh, I don't recall – oh, wait!" Thomas let out a quiet chuckle. "Eustace kept his school grades in it, didn't he?"

Joseph hit Thomas on the back lovingly, but rather firmly. "That he did!"

Thomas now remembered why Eustace kept his grades in the diary. "He liked to show his friends – well, I suppose friends would be the wrong word here – he liked to compare his grades with others, to show them that he had done better." Thomas stopped speaking and looked Joseph in the eyes. "I get it. It was about him. It was all about him. Eustace didn't even care about the grades, he just used them as proof that he was better."

"Yes, my friend, but he changed. He changed." Joseph's words echoed with meaning and depth. Thomas waited, knowing that the wisdom shared by this man was a gift. He let the words repeat in his mind, hoping to hold on to as much as he was capable.

"Thomas, we find many ways to avoid making the changes we know we must make, avoid changing our lives for the better. As an example, many people don't – or maybe the appropriate word is won't – read the Bible today. Why? In their hearts, they know it will challenge them to change, to grow. It won't let them continue to walk an easy path. So many don't dig into their spiritual beliefs. They do so for a very simple reason. It would challenge them to change, to confront. Surely, Thomas, you recall our last conversation about David and Goliath?"

Thomas nodded, feeling the weight of his friend's words. Thomas was not resisting this message. He knew that this lesson was one he needed.

"Most of us are all too familiar with that story. But, my friend, knowing the story and letting the story affect you... these are very different matters. David confronted Goliath. You and I, we each must confront our Goliaths. They are always there. In every story, in every relationship, in every life. But all too often we ignore them, or run from them. Some of us do this through busyness. We lead complicated lives to avoid changing them, to avoid facing Goliath. *'Human history*,' our wise friend C.S. Lewis said, '*is the long terrible story of man trying to find something other than God which will make him happy.*' That, Thomas, was certainly true for me throughout most of my life. That was my Goliath. Sure, I've had many since then, but that was a big one and I avoided it for much, much too long." Thomas could see a brief flash of sadness in his friend's face; but in an instant, the sadness was gone. It was replaced with joy.

Joseph continued. "Have you heard the expression, Thomas, '*nemo dat quod non habet*'?" Thomas shook his head in awe. His friend was at it again! Joseph translated. "*You can't give what you don't have.* Thomas, many years ago, I made a decision. It was a Goliath decision. Let God affect you and, as a result, let your life affect others. That was my decision. I was still very early in my spiritual journey when I made this decision, but I knew it was right. Not long after making this decision – which, of course was much easier to make than to live out – I began to explore C.S. Lewis' works. I stumbled over his perspective in so many ways. I'd read a quote here, see a friend reading one of his books, or hear him referenced in a lecture. Thomas, as I read more from this towering spiritual intellect, I wanted to know more about his story. When I read of his deep conversations with another literary giant, J.R.R. Tolkien, I started to face another Goliath. You see, Tolkien was a mentor for Lewis when it mattered most. I started asking myself if I should develop the knowledge, wisdom, metaphors, communication skills necessary to be a Tolkien to a future Lewis? Could I – or would I – be willing to mentor, advise, debate, someone like Lewis? That idea became another of my Goliaths. Does this make sense, Thomas?"

Thomas was sitting completely still, staring across the river. He had to remind himself to take a breath and quietly replied, "It does. It makes perfect sense."

"Thomas, I don't have all the answers. I used to think I did, or that I was supposed to."

Thomas laughed, and thought to himself, No! Does even Joseph get caught by '*supposed*' to?

Joseph's stood up, took a few steps towards the water, and then turned to Thomas. "Love is a choice; a choice that requires a price, that requires sacrifice. If you only choose love when it's easy, that's not love. Real love often hurts." He stopped speaking and Thomas could see these were more than mere words for Joseph. He finally continued, "Thomas, I don't know what you should do with your assistant coach, was it Ben?"

"Yes, Ben."

Joseph was slowly walking back and forth now. "You can't lead, truly lead, without love. You can help Ben. But expect it to hurt. And it will likely hurt both of you. Removing him from his position or cutting him from the team might be the right answer. Whatever you decide to do should be done to help him become the young man he's capable of becoming. That process is rarely easy."

Joseph stopped walking and looked at Thomas, who was now standing next to their familiar green bench.

"Recall, young Thomas, our recent discussion about Eustace's attempts to change from a Dragon back to a boy. You may be surprised at what you will find if you will read that section of the book again. Eustace couldn't make the change all by himself. And the change wasn't as sudden as we often find in fairy tales."

The two friends stood side by side for what seemed several minutes. Nothing was said. Nothing needed to be.

Before they parted, Thomas embraced his friend, and said softly but very firmly, "Thank you. You are a gift. Your words and guidance are gifts. Thank you, my friend."

Again!

Tiff surprised Thomas by inviting all of the camp staff to her place to celebrate the conclusion of a successful baseball summer camp. Everyone showed up and, after several hours of great food, conversation, and even a good toast by Coach Thomas, most of the guests had gone home. Clara and Joey stuck around to help clean up. Both Tiff and Clara expressed their congratulations to Thomas for what he had accomplished. Thomas humbly replied, "Thanks! I know now – really a better way to put it would be I'm just starting to realize – that it's just the beginning. But that's okay. Better questions lead to better answers." His voice trailed off and his last sentence seemed to be meant more for himself than for another. "What are you looking for, indeed!"

The three sat together and watched, while Joey and Ryan were absorbed in some imaginary adventure. A warm breeze rustled through the trees.

Joey quietly walked over to Thomas and tapped on his hand, politely getting his coach's attention.

"What is it, buddy?" Thomas gave the little guy a serious look and his complete attention.

"Well, Coach, Ryan told me about the books you read with him. About Narnia and Aslan. We were just playing a game about it." As he spoke, Ryan came over to join the group, hopped up on his mother's lap, and was listening intently. Joey continued, "Will you read them to me?" His face glowed with anticipation and hope.

All eyes were on Joey, or they might have noticed a moistness in Tiff's eyes, accompanied by a smile of pure joy.

Ryan's voice suddenly rang loud through the quiet evening, "Uncle Tommy! Uncle Tommy!" He had the attention of the whole group and he continued, at a slightly lower volume, but the excitement flowed out of him and resonated in his words. "Can we? I mean can we read them again? Together – with Joey? Could we,

Uncle Tommy?" After a glance from his mother, he added, "Please?"

"Yes, Ryan, we can read them all over again. Together."

About the Author

Jonathan Fanning is the author of several books, including his best-selling book (*Who are you BECOMING?*), and has inspired and challenged audiences with his message around the world. He speaks for companies, non-profits, educational organizations, and churches. Jonathan was voted the best speaker at a recent TED conference. A traumatic car accident and several other "Frying Pan" moments in the middle of Fanning's career as a management consultant launched a quest for a deeper sense of purpose, meaning, and significance. *"Who are you BECOMING?"* and *"Who are you helping the people around you to BECOME?"* became central to Jonathan's life, business, and speaking. He has built several successful businesses, including a national children's fitness franchise and Entrepreneur Adventure, which helps young people experience business start-up and ownership. Jonathan lives in NY with his wife, Dominika, and daughters, Ella and Maya.

Jonathan's popular speeches and workshops include:
- *Who are you BECOMING?*
- *Creative Leadership: Building a Culture of Innovation*
- *They Serve: The Essence of Authentic Leadership*
- *Developing Emotional Intelligence*
- *Leadership (and Life) Lessons from Legends*

For more information and engaging videos, visit us online:
www.JonathanFanning.com

Made in the USA
Middletown, DE
27 August 2023

37256331R00104